Dissimiles:
More's the Pity

by

Wesley Payton

Downstate Illinois Series, Book 3

Dissimiles: More's the Pity

COPYRIGHT © 2022 by Wesley Payton

Cover Art by *Debbie Taylor*

The Wild Rose Press, Inc.
PO Box 708
Adams Basin, NY 14410-0708
Visit us at www.thewildrosepress.com

Publishing History
First Edition, 2022
Trade Paperback ISBN 978-1-5092-4315-0
Digital ISBN 978-1-5092-4316-7

Downstate Illinois Series, Book 3
Published in the United States of America

Weston knelt to pick up his shrimp off the floor.

"Oh, you needn't bother with that." The woman pointed toward a uniformed man approaching with a dustpan. "The catering crew will take care of it."

"But it's my mess."

"I think more accurately it's our mess, but it's his job." The woman helped Weston up. "Come to the bar and have a drink with me, so as to give this man space to ply his trade."

"I feel a bit guilty about not helping, but I suppose a glass of whiskey might assuage my shame."

"I hope you don't think me a supercilious heiress who considers cleaning floors beneath her—you know, figuratively. I just feel it's rude to presume to do another's work. After all, how would you feel if someone took over writing your Spinster stories?"

Weston motioned to the bartender. "A bourbon on the rocks for me and a…chardonnay, for the lady?"

"The lady will have a bourbon too," she said.

Weston smiled at the heiress as the bartender poured the whiskey over ice. "So we know each other without ever having met."

The heiress took the glasses from the bartender and handed one to Weston. "I was up most of last night rereading *Saturnine Spinster*. Your work is very comforting…like literary mac and cheese."

Dedication

For my friends Scott, Todd, Carrie, Cory, Kara, and Micah. I miss those summers home from college spent night fishing.

Dedication

Prologue

The photographer's tungsten studio lights made Weston feel like an old cheeseburger under a heat lamp. "Are you sure they didn't put too much makeup on me? I think all this warpaint is starting to melt."

"You look very lifelike," said H.P.

"And you look like a damn rodeo clown."

"I feel rather clownish for having agreed to this ridiculous photoshoot instead of just insisting that they use our separate headshots for the book jacket, and certainly a rodeo clown is apt, considering how much of your bullshit I've had to put up with these last few months."

"What are you talking about? I'm a dream to work with."

"Then I'm hoping like most of my dreams, I soon forget all about it."

The fey photographer took yet another camera from his assistant. "Okay you two, let's have you both get on the floor, and we'll try something a little unconventional."

As H.P. started to get down on his hands and knees, Weston raised an objection. "I've done a bunch of these shoots over the years, and usually I'm in and out in under twenty minutes—quicker than a haircut."

"Darling, I'm not a barber…I'm a stylist. Put your trust in me, and I promise you'll be pleased with the

1

results. Now lie on the floor with your heads together—this isn't a wrestling match."

The two did as they were instructed, with equal parts grumbling and popping joints.

"You know, I think our publisher had something more traditional in mind," Weston said, "along the lines of a yearbook photo…or a mug shot."

The photographer adjusted his lens. "So pedestrian…so prosaic."

"Well, we are prose writers," added H.P.

"Not in my pictures—I will make you look like artists."

His adjustment completed, the photographer stepped one foot over their heads, straddling H.P. and Weston as he focused his camera directly above them.

"Jesus, I'm glad you're not wearing a kilt." Weston rolled his head back and forth on the floor. "I can't remember the last time I felt this uncomfortable."

"I can," H.P. said, "the day after your bachelor party."

"No more talking," ordered the photographer. "Be silent and still…simply let the moment wash over you."

"Oh, I'm definitely going to wash myself after this," said Weston.

Chapter 1

Kate looked up from an electron microscope as her lab assistant gathered his things to leave for the day. "I appreciate you preparing all these samples with the microtome today—each is a little slice of heaven."

"Not exactly the sort of cutting-edge work that I thought I'd be doing here," said the young man, "but I guess it beats scrubbing down the crosslinker."

"Your time will come…a biome isn't built in a day."

"Thanks Dr. Kate." He opened the glass-and-steel door to exit the cleanroom. "Don't stay too late."

When Kate heard the heavy door click shut, she powered off her microscope and opened her laptop. She returned to a partially composed email. She'd written and rewritten it many times over the past few days but had yet to actually send it. After rereading it once again, she added: *In conclusion, I don't doubt that your intentions are noble, but I'm reminded of another Nobel man, who despite being a pacifist, left behind a legacy of destruction due to his invention of dynamite, which he'd originally developed to improve the safety of mining operations. I understand that because you created this company you think you can control it, but people die, whereas companies can effectively be immortal. We must never forget that while it's possible to invent many things, it's impossible to uninvent anything.*

Kate took a deep breath and sent the email. Then she opened another email and began typing: *Eddie, I'm leaving work soon and headed to Union Station— looking forward to meeting up with you and your friends later tonight. XOXO*

She clicked Send, wishing she could call Edwin directly or even text him, rather than sending him an email that he wouldn't see until he was in front of a computer screen. For the umpteenth time, Kate considered buying Edwin a mobile phone, even though he'd expressly told her on several occasions that he didn't want one. *Maybe if I got him a Fantastic Four case to go along with it.* She searched online for cellphone covers, placing a couple of contenders in her shopping cart. Then she took note of the time and closed the laptop.

Kate scanned her lab. Satisfied that all was in its proper place, she crossed toward the door to turn off the lights, but before she reached the switch, the lab was cast into darkness. Then she heard the lab door click open.

A flashlight beam swept across the lab.

Kate instinctively dropped down to the floor as the person holding the light entered the room. She didn't hear the familiar sound caused by the friction of cleanroom coveralls, like plastic corduroy, as the person moved about the lab. She thought perhaps a new janitor, unfamiliar with the cleanroom protocols, had entered the wrong room by mistake, but then realized she also didn't hear the telltale sound of jangling keys, so she remained silent and crawled toward the door.

Reaching the end of the long table closest to the

exit, Kate waited and watched as the beam of light moved toward the far side of the lab. She wouldn't be able to open the heavy door without giving away her position, but she figured she'd have just enough time to get through the door and lock it behind her before whoever was holding the flashlight could cross the dark room—or at least she hoped so.

As the beam swept past the autoclave against the far wall, Kate leapt from her crouched position toward the door and tugged at the handle.

It didn't budge.

She'd been locked in—trapped. She turned as the beam from the flashlight shined on her face. She squinted in the brightness. "Who are you…a custodian?"

"In a manner of speaking," replied the man holding the flashlight. "I am paid to clean up messes—that is, me and my associate."

Kate heard the door click open behind her. She twisted around to see the electric blue glow of a Taser in the darkness.

Chapter 2

Weston entered the house with a bucket of fried chicken and a container of mashed potatoes.

Van and Lance briefly looked up from the video game they were playing on the living room television, and then just as quickly returned their attention to the screen.

"I thought we were having Thai tonight," said Van.

"That was the plan, but the Thai place keeps closing earlier and earlier—at this rate, it'll be a lunch-only restaurant by springtime." Weston crossed to the dining room and set dinner on the table.

"But I wanted rice noodles," said Lance, talking more to the TV than to Weston.

"And I wanted a 'how was your day' when I walked through the door, but you play the cards you're dealt."

Ance tentatively toddled into the living room, gripping Becky's thumbs for support.

"My Becca and my baby," said Weston. "Aren't you two ambulatory beauties a joy to behold?"

"This little joy just spit up grape juice on my favorite Dixie Chicks T-shirt."

"That's what children do—bring new joy into your life while simultaneously eradicating past pleasures."

"Pa da," cooed Ance.

Weston picked up his daughter. "No sweetie, I'm

either Papa or Dada."

"I think she's hungry," said Becky. "I believe she was trying to say Pad See Ew."

"It's good to see you too." Weston kissed his wife. "Okay boys, it's time for dinner, so finish defending the Earth or crushing each other's skulls and then turn off the TV."

Becky set the table as Weston buckled Ance into her high chair. "Only a year old, and you're already sitting at the head of the table."

Van and Lance took their usual seats opposite each other as Weston and Becky sat down on either side of the high chair. Becky placed a dollop of mashed potatoes on Ance's tray as Weston took a drumstick and passed the chicken bucket to Van.

"I heard a good joke today," said Lance. "Knock, knock."

"Who cares," replied Van.

Lance shook his head. "No, you're supposed to say, 'who's there?'"

"Buddy, I think Van is trying to tell you that knock-knock jokes are a little jejune," said Weston. "And I think he might be right…after all, you're going into junior high next year."

"But most of the jokes I know are knock-knocks."

"Here's one that's sure to kill in junior high," said Van. "It's a classic at 4-H. So this farmer is trying to teach his cousin from the city how to milk a cow, and he says 'milking a cow is just like jerking off—'"

"Van!" Becky leveled a baleful look at her oldest son. "Inappropriate for so many reasons."

"What? There's no cuss words in it."

"Oh, is that the one where the guy tells the farmer,

'So I have to show the cow naked pictures of your wife on the Internet?'" asked Lance. "Yeah, I don't really get it."

"That's good." Becky tousled her youngest son's hair. "You just stick to your knocker jokes...I think they're funny."

"If you want, I can tell you some really funny jokes about knockers later," Van added.

"Vancy, you'll do no such thing," said Becky. "I need you two to stop being so unruly...instead, for a change of pace, try being ruly—now eat your chicken."

Lance held up a thoroughly gnawed leg bone. "But I'm out of chicken. Can I have another drumstick?"

Weston looked inside the bucket. "Sorry, there's no more drumsticks. There's a thigh and a pair of b—or how about a wing?"

"I'll take the thigh," Lance answered.

Weston set the piece of chicken on the boy's plate, and everyone resumed eating. The ensuing silence was interrupted by inharmonious abdominal noises emanating from Weston's person. "I don't think this greasy chicken is agreeing with me."

"It doesn't sound so much like a disagreement but rather a full-on argument," Becky replied.

"I think it sounds like whale song," said Lance.

Van shook his head. "No, it sounds like a fat guy trying to climb out of a wet innertube."

"That's very vivid," complimented Weston. "I hope you're using some of that talent for imagery in your college-application essays, though be careful not to overdo it with the similes."

"What about dissimiles?" Van asked. "I mean, if similes help you visualize something by relating it to something else that's similar, wouldn't dissimiles be equally as helpful for picturing something that's dissimilar—you know, compare and contrast?"

"Can you give us an example?" asked Becky.

"When somebody says something 'is as cold as ice' I wonder why they didn't just stop at cold, since something being as cold as ice doesn't really make a strong impression, but if they told me something is so cold it feels like the opposite of lava—well, I think that's more memorable because it requires a little bit of imagination."

"I get what you're getting at," said Weston, "but I don't think employing 'dissimiles' would benefit your cause in a college essay."

"Isn't my 'cause' to demonstrate that I have a unique perspective? I can't remember the last time I read a dissimile, and I bet it's the same for whoever reads those stupid essays."

"I suspect there's a good reason for that," replied Weston. "Doing something that isn't often done could be considered unique, but more often than not it's considered unwise. Take the so-called music that you're so fond of; rap is riddled with similes, but I've never once heard BMX or Dr. Jay use a dissimile."

"What's wrong with rap music?" asked Lance.

"You mean besides that it's not music?"

"You're not that old," said Van. "They must've had rap music when you were my age."

"They did, but back then it was fun, and you could dance to it. Nowadays, it's all just a bunch of people bitching or bragging."

"You were saying the same thing about social media last week," said Lance. "I remember because

Mom doesn't like anybody using the word for a female dog, but for some reason I guess it's okay for you to use the word, uh, female dogging."

Becky looked up from helping Ance with her potatoes. "He's got you there."

Weston sighed. "Buddy, you're probably right. I shouldn't use the word b—female dogging, but I think my point still stands."

Van rolled his eyes so hard that Weston was mildly concerned the boy might detach his retinas. "What point is that…back in your day everything was better?"

"I'd never say that. Some things were better…others were worse."

"Were family dinners better?" Lance asked. "You know, fewer bad jokes and less female dogging?"

Weston took a drink of water. "You likely won't believe me until you're over the hill like I am, but nothing is better than this. I ate a lot of dinners alone when I was your age. My mom often had to work late, and my father was mostly out of the picture."

"Did he have a problem with drugs like our dad?" Van asked.

"No, he had different kinds of problems. When I was six, he left to go buy a pack of cigarettes, and I didn't see him again until I was a teenager."

"Sounds like he got lost," said Lance.

"That's a good way to put it."

Becky reached across the table to hold Weston's hand. "I'm sorry, hon."

"It's all right—saved me from years of secondhand smoke. Listen boys, I'm certain that when your dad finishes with his treatment program, he's going to put his life back together and be the kind of father I wish

I'd had."

"What makes you so sure?" asked Van.

"Because he's got the two best reasons in the world for doing so."

Van grinned. "I get what you're getting at."

Chapter 3

Weston knocked on the front door of H.P.'s old farmhouse. He heard footsteps within and soon H.P. stood in the open doorway wearing a natty tweed coat.

"It's radio," said Weston. "Why are you wearing a jacket?"

"A blazer is the de rigueur dress code for teachers on campus."

"But you're only an instructor, not a full-fledged professor, so couldn't you get away with just a vest?"

H.P. momentarily looked as if he were considering slamming the door in Weston's face. "I won't bother asking that you promise not to embarrass me tonight as I know it's not within your power to keep such a promise, but please don't feel as if every snide remark you make during our little interview this evening has to be at my expense."

"You're welcome, by the way, for me driving all the way out here to pick you up."

"And you're welcome for me writing almost the entirety our book."

"I wrote the beginning," Weston objected.

"You mean the two-page prologue that didn't have anything to do with the rest of the story that followed? Yes, bravo."

"I came up with some of the ideas."

"Ideas are what books are about, but words are

what books are made of."

"I'll make it up to you on the next one."

"There not being a 'next one' will be thanks enough." H.P. moved out of the doorway. "Come on in for a minute. I need to shut down my computer and turn off some lights upstairs."

H.P. ascended to the attic as Weston toured the living room, which looked to him more like a junk store. He picked up two telescope eyepieces from an end table and held them to his eyes like binoculars, moving one closer to his face as he moved the other farther away. Then he put them back down, as he felt a slight headache coming on.

"You all right there?" H.P. entered from the kitchen. "You look like someone who drank a milkshake too quickly."

"I was just in the middle of a profound and original thought. It doesn't surprise me that you're unfamiliar with how that looks."

"Well let's get going before your head explodes all over my area rug."

Weston glanced at the floor. "I didn't even notice a rug down there, what with it being covered by all these telescope pieces and star charts."

H.P. sighed. "Yes, Edwin has effectively taken over my living room, as you can plainly see."

"I thought he and Kate were cohabitating these days."

"Only part-time. He can't stay there for more than a few days in a row…misses his stargazing, and it seems there's too much light pollution at her place just outside Chicago. Luckily for him, my backyard happens to be a perfect spot for starwatching. Unluckily for me, my living room happens to be a perfect spot for storing all his astronomy gear."

"I didn't realize he was borrowing your car to drive back and forth so frequently."

"He's not. He usually takes the train, which is like heaven on rails for him. He just borrowed my car tonight to pick up Kate from the train station. They're going to meet us after the broadcast at the Faculty Lounge."

Weston eyed a framed movie poster for *The Million Dollar Mermaid* as they moved toward the door. "I thought Ethel Merman, not Esther Williams, was the Mermaid."

"Why, because her last name was Merman?"

"No," Weston answered defensively, "I suppose I got them confused because Ethel and Ester sound so much alike."

"You know Billie Holiday wasn't in *Holiday Inn* either, right?"

"Stow it."

H.P. locked the door behind them. "Or Michael Caine in *The Caine Mutiny,* for that matter?"

"You are aware that there have been movies made in our lifetime, aren't you? A guy who looks as old as you doesn't need to try so hard to prove he's out of touch."

Chapter 4

Weston and H.P. sat on two small, metal chairs in the cluttered college-radio broadcast booth. "I think my old dorm room on campus was bigger than this place," Weston said.

"If the quarters are too claustrophobic for your liking, you're welcome to wait out in the hallway," replied H.P. "I'll wave at you through the window if I require your assistance describing the book I wrote almost single-handedly."

Weston shook his head. "No, I caught the last one of these interviews you did. I think you need me in here…you did not come off well."

A youthful economics professor that H.P. had only met once before entered the booth. "Hey you two, as you probably know I've been filling in as the host for Tuesday Night Talks for the past several months."

"Your parents must be very proud," said Weston. "Is your intention to one day attend school here as well?"

The young man pushed at the bridge of his brightly colored glasses. "No, I teach econ…you're just messing with me, aren't you?"

"Don't mind him," said H.P. "He's one of those surly fellows who's always cross because he can't come up with a good excuse for being such a churl."

"Ah…a hater." The smooth-faced professor sat

behind his microphone on the other side of the table and leaned back in his ergonomically designed chair. "Your publisher mailed an Advanced Reader Copy of your book. I didn't have a chance to read it all, but I gave it a good perusing, so I think I get the gist of the story."

"I didn't realize they'd printed the ARCs yet," H.P. said. "May I have a look?"

"Of course." The host slid the book across the table. "In fact, I was hoping you two would sign it for me. If you would, please make it out to 'Dear eBay Customer'…see, I like to make jokes too. I doubt I'd get very much for it anyway."

H.P. turned the book over and then showed Weston the back cover.

Weston let out a cough. "After all that rolling around on the floor, they went ahead and used our damn headshots."

The producer gave a signal from the other side of the glass, and the host said, "Okay, it looks like we're on in five."

"Good," Weston replied. "My throat's a little dry, so I'm going to get a quick drink of—"

"No," interrupted H.P. "Take five is in minutes, on in five is in seconds."

"Welcome to another installment of Tuesday Night Talks. In the booth with me this evening is one of our very own creative-writing instructors, known affectionally to his colleagues and students as H.P."

"Good to be with you all again tonight."

"And next to him sits another local writer who has co-authored a new novel with H.P.—one Mr. Weston Payley."

Weston opened his mouth, began to speak, and

instead hacked into his microphone. His hacking soon crescendoed into a full-blown coughing fit.

H.P. pulled on his earlobe. "Well said, Weston."

The host signaled the producer as he moved closer to his microphone. "Since we've gotten the introductions out of the way, I think now would be a good time for a word from one of our sponsors."

****

"We're back, and I believe sufficiently hydrated," said the host. "Weston, you were saying something I found particularly interesting during the break about how the game show *Wheel of Fortune* is both like a simile and a dissimile for our contemporary American experience."

"Uh, I didn't realize we were going to talk about this on air." Weston took a drink from a bottle of water.

"As a professor of economics, I found your comments fascinating, and I believe our audience would agree."

"All right…it wasn't any sort of deep insight. I just happened to notice someone watching *Wheel* in the breakroom, and it occurred to me that the show is similar to the process of attaining wealth in our society, since whoever has the most money at the end of the game gets to go onto the bonus round. I mean wouldn't it be fairer if whoever came in last got a chance to win the extra money?"

"A compelling observation, I'd say. And now if you would indulge us further by sharing your musings on how the game show is a dissimile or antilogue, so to speak, if you'll forgive my continuation on your riff."

"I'll forgive you for everything except suggesting that I'm some sort of muser…but sure, *Wheel of*

Fortune is unlike real life in that all the contestants on the show start out with the same amount of money. The situation in this room would be a more accurate simulacrum…everyone gets a seat at the table—just some of the seats are upholstered and others are folding."

The host swiveled in his chair. "H.P., what do you think of your co-author's comparison?"

Weston cleared his throat. "One last thing I'd like to add along those same lines before we move on is that as the gulf between the poor who feel they're owed and the rich who feel they're entitled expands, the distance between our society and the death of civility will shrink. Go ahead and remember I said that."

"Okay," H.P. replied, "now if only we knew why you said that. However, Weston's perspective—such as it is—runs parallel to the point of view of a character, albeit a minor one, from our new book."

"Pardon," said Weston, "I promise, final interruption before we delve into the book, but I feel as if we're all having a real simpatico moment here, so I'd like the listeners out there to consider something if they would: life is more difficult for some than others. If you happen to be one of the fortunate few for whom life is easier, then you should count your blessings and refrain from telling those who've suffered misfortune to simply 'look on the bright side.'"

"While I think many of my listeners likely appreciate your sentiment, I feel as if we're drifting into didacticism."

H.P. shook his head. "Drifting? I think we've paddled right over the waterfall, so before we get too far downriver, I'd be remiss if I didn't inform your audience that our book isn't heavy-handed at all but rather more of a breezy, entertaining type read."

"Well," said Weston, "maybe your part of the story."

"My part? I'm Jack Kirby to your Stan Lee."

"That's patently absurd. Firstly, nobody knows what the hell you're talking about, and thirdly, I find your accusation to be as spurious as your analogy is specious."

"And I find you to be a sphincter…and Payley absurd."

The host pointed to his producer. "Perhaps it's time for another commercial break."

****

"And we're back again. So I understand that you two will embark on a globe-trotting book tour beginning very soon to drum up interest in advance of your novel's release."

"More regional than global," H.P. clarified, "but yes, our first stop is in Indianapolis this Saturday."

"Indiana?" Weston moaned.

"Correct, that's where Indianapolis is located these days," replied H.P.

"What's the point of going there?"

"I take it you're not a fan of the Hoosier State," said the host.

"In my youth, I liked the gals over there just fine. 'But, Mama, he pulled a nickel from behind my ear…I thought that meant we was married,'" said Weston in a derogatorily imitative voice. "But trying to sell books to hosers is like trying to sell toboggans to Bedouins…or dissimilarly, unlike trying to sell igloos to Innuits. In short, it's a fool's errand."

19

H.P. turned to Weston. "In that case, one of us is definitely the right man for the job."

"Weston, I like your call back to dissimiles," the host said. "So are you implying that our neighbors to the east live in a cultural wasteland?"

"No, I wouldn't go that far. Indianapolis is home to a first-rate children's museum, or as the benighted locals refer to it: The Museum."

"Could you just stop talking for one damn minute?" pleaded H.P. "We were better off when you were coughing out your lungs into the microphone."

"What are you getting so worked up about? Are you really afraid that illiterate Indianans are going to lift their statewide ban on books, suddenly learn how to read en masse, and then not buy our novel?"

****

"H.P., I'd like to give you the final word," said the host.

"Gee thanks, if I add that one to the other couple that I've managed to get in edgewise tonight, maybe they'll all amount to a complete sentence."

"What would you say the key is to writing an engaging story?"

"The trick to good storytelling is to live your life— things will happen, pick the ones that stand out, digest them for a decade or two, changing almost every detail along the way, and then there you go."

"That sounds familiar to me," said Weston.

"Yeah, my mentor back in Chicago used to say something similar."

"Your mentor…you mean that crazy old coot who was a habitué of the bar you worked at?"

"You know he's dead now, right?"

Weston frowned. "Too bad…he was a helluva guy. But Fashion Glasses asked for your final word—not some barfly's."

"I've got a few choice words that I'd like to share with you right now, though I think the FCC might take exception to them."

"I'm sorry, gentlemen," the host said. "I'm afraid that's the end of our show—but sincerely, thank you for coming. I can't remember the last time we had a more spirited discussion in this studio. Please do come back again soon…the both of you—together."

Chapter 5

As H.P. and Weston entered the Faculty Lounge, many a pint glass was raised in their honor. The pair took the only open stools at the bar.

"Is it always so lively in here?" asked Weston.

"No," H.P. answered, "especially not on a Tuesday."

"You seem to be quite popular."

The bartender approached. "What can I get you two?"

"A scotch rocks for me," H.P. said, "and a double Jeppson's Malört neat for him."

"Belay that last order, my good barman." Weston reached for his wallet. "I'll have a scotch, too."

The bartender held up his palm. "Your money's no good here tonight."

"Why's his money no good?" asked H.P.

"We listened to the broadcast...had us in stitches," answered the bartender. "All the laughs were great for business."

H.P. looked around the bar. "Everyone here heard tonight's radio show?"

"You bet—piped it in through the stereo speakers since your last one was so entertaining." The bartender set two glasses on the bar. "Funny stuff...though you never really come off well in those things."

H.P. glared at Weston. "Gosh, I had no idea."

"What are you looking at me for? Tonight was my first time doing one of those; that last one was on you."

H.P. turned to the bartender. "Has Edwin been in?"

"I haven't seen him, but then it's a big crowd tonight." The bartender filled both their glasses with ice and then poured scotch over them. "Besides, he usually doesn't start ordering drinks until somebody else shows up to pay for them."

As if on cue, Edwin walked through the door, his face marked with concern as he approached H.P. and Weston. "Have either of you seen Kate?"

"No," answered H.P. "I thought you were picking her up at the train station."

"That was our plan, but the train got in late, and she wasn't on it. I thought maybe she caught an earlier one and came here."

"Do you want to use my phone to call her?" Weston handed Edwin his mobile phone.

"Thank you. I stopped at a couple of places I thought might have a pay phone, but they're becoming ever more difficult to find these days." Edwin tapped in her number on the screen and then held the phone to his ear for a few moments. "Kate, it's me. I missed you at the train station. Give me a call at this number—it's Weston's phone—to let me know where you are. Take care."

Weston took his phone back. "Take care?"

"What's wrong with take care?" asked Edwin.

"There's nothing wrong with it per se, but it's what I usually tell the delivery guy after I tip him."

"I think the romance writer is suggesting that you ought to consider closing your messages with something a bit more familiar," said H.P.

"Like what?"

"How do you say goodbye in person?" asked Weston.

"I give her a hug and then say: take care."

"You're a hopeless romantic," said Weston. "Or maybe just hopeless."

H.P. patted Edwin on his shoulder. "At least he hugs her rather than shaking her hand."

Weston's phone vibrated. He held it up to look at the screen. "It's a text from Kate: Ed, got delayed…see you tomorrow—OX OX."

"What's with the oxen?" asked H.P.

"Sorry, I misread it." Weston looked again at the text. "I imagine she meant hugs and kisses."

"No, something's wrong." Edwin looked at the screen. "She never calls me Ed, and she always ends her messages with XOXO."

"That is better than 'take care,'" said Weston.

Edwin frowned. "I'm serious. In all things, from research to missives, Kate is meticulous…it's what I adore most about her. I think she's in trouble."

Chapter 6

"Still no answer?" Weston asked as he drove Edwin and H.P. toward the interstate. Edwin shook his head as he put Weston's phone in the cupholder between them. "Do you want to try her neighbor again in the next condo to see if she made it home yet?"

"No," answered Edwin. "Kate's a creature of habit like me. She would've been home hours ago if that's where she went."

"Can you use my phone to track hers?"

"How do you do that?"

"I have no idea, but I've seen it done in movies."

"You could try to ping it," H.P. said from the backseat.

"How do you do that?" Edwin asked again.

"I'm not sure," H.P. answered. "I imagine it involves pinging—whatever that is."

"I can't track her phone, but I think I might be able to track her car." Edwin turned to H.P. "Can you hand me the laptop from my backpack?"

"You're in your fifties; I think it might be time to upgrade to a briefcase or maybe a satchel." H.P. rummaged around in the pack. "I take it back…aside from your laptop, this thing is full of candy and comic books. I suppose a backpack that looks like it might belong to a kid is completely appropriate."

Edwin took the computer from H.P. "It's not my

laptop. It's Kate's personal computer, but I use it more than she does since she's always on her work computer. Anyway, her car has one of those plug-in insurance devices that tracks her mileage and such. I suspect her account's password is saved on this computer." Edwin opened the laptop and executed a series of keystrokes. "Eureka…according to the last update, her car is still at work."

"Mightn't that mean that she's still working?" asked H.P. "Maybe she was delayed, as she mentioned in her text, by whatever she's working on and turned off her cellphone to limit distractions."

"Or her car may be there," said Weston, "but she could've gotten a ride with someone else and doesn't want to take any calls at the moment."

Edwin considered both possibilities and several others, but it only strengthened his resolve. "No, she's in trouble. I just know somehow…it's like those hunches you always get."

Weston glanced over at Edwin. "I hear you Ed, but as you well know—half the time my hunches turn out to be wrong."

"And even when they are, I still support you."

Weston returned his eyes to the road. "It looks like we're Chicagoing."

H.P. leaned forward. "There are 106 miles to Chicago, we have a full tank of gas, half a pack of cigarettes, it's dark, and we're wearing sunglasses."

"I'd estimate that it's closer to 140 miles," said Edwin. "And no one in this car smokes."

"That reminds me, I should stop and fuel up." Weston looked at H.P. in the rearview mirror. "If you want, you can go inside the gas station and buy yourself a pair of sunglasses."

"You two really know how to ruin *The Blues Brothers* vibe."

"I can try to find some blues music on the radio," Weston said.

"I think I have a theremin CD in my backpack," offered Edwin.

Chapter 7

Weston noticed a decrease in buildings along the interstate and an increase in the distances between exit ramps. "When you told me that Kate worked in the suburbs, I thought you meant like Schaumburg or something. We're hell and gone from the city and damn near back into the hinterlands."

"Her company's compound is located just off the next exit," said Edwin. "It's pretty much the only thing out there."

"Compound?" asked H.P. "I was imagining a lab in some facility affiliated with a university."

"The compound houses multiple labs. The way I understand it, her company doesn't exactly have affiliations…only clients with deep pockets." Edwin pointed to a sign for the upcoming exit. "That's it—one more mile."

"So is this compound the company's headquarters?" Weston asked.

"As far as I know, it's the whole company. They like to have everyone under one roof—or rather within one perimeter fence—to keep their scientists from being siloed so that new ideas can cross-pollinate between the various departments. Also, since there's not much competition for the land out this far from the city, they can expand as necessary, which it seems they've been doing by leaps and bounds over the past few years."

"I imagine, given Kate's line of work, that they must have a number of sensitive projects underway at any given time," said H.P. "Security is likely easier to ensure if everything is in a single, isolated location."

Weston steered toward the exit ramp. "If it's such a secure compound, are they just going to let us drive up and knock on the front door of Kate's building?"

"Rather than going through the rigmarole of having a guest pass issued to me each time I come out here to visit her, Kate got me set up with consultant credentials by having me help out with a few of her studies. That won't get us inside her secure lab, but at least it'll get us past the guard at the front gate."

"Studies?" H.P. asked. "Are you letting your neuroscientist girlfriend experiment on your brain?"

"Of course not, I merely review some of the findings from tests her lab assistants conduct. I assure you it's all rather mundane and quite innocuous."

Weston shook his head as he pulled up to the gatehouse. "Yeah, that sounds just like what the guy in a horror movie says right before he finds out that they've cloned an evil twin of him who can kill with a thought."

"Could you two keep your decidedly unscientific nonsense to yourselves while I talk to the guard?"

Weston rolled down his window as the guard approached. The chill of the night air entered the car as the young guard bent to look inside.

Edwin leaned over the center console. "Quincy, is it?"

"No sir, it's Quinten. You always say my name wrong."

"Sorry about that. I went to school with a Quincy."

"You always say that too. Sort of late for a visit, isn't it? All the labs are closed for the night."

"I know, but Kate thought she might've dropped her cellphone in the parking lot, so I told her I'd come try to find it for her."

The guard looked at H.P. in the backseat. "I see you brought some friends to help."

"Many eyes make for a shorter search," replied Edwin. "Or at least I hope so."

"Okay, come on through then. Let me know on your way back out if you didn't find it, and I'll have all the guards during the shift change in the morning take a quick look."

"Much appreciated," Edwin replied as the guard pushed a button to open the gate.

Weston drove past the gatehouse. "I sometimes think mobile phones were only invented so that searching for lost ones could be used as a pretext for snooping around. So where am I going?"

"Just take a left and keep driving. Her lab is in the third building, and she has her own spot out front."

"Personal parking space," H.P. said, "very nice."

"What, the university doesn't give you your own parking spot?" asked Weston.

"You've seen the size of my office. I think the university figures I'd find it insulting if they gave my car more space on campus than me."

Edwin pointed to the parking lot of the third building. "Her spot's the closest non-handicapped space near the door."

"Okay, Ed," replied Weston. "The lot's completely empty. Do you want me turn around and head back the way we came, or do you want me to pull in so that we can make a show of looking for a pretend phone in case the guard makes his rounds, and before you answer, let me remind you that it's cold out there?"

"Pull in," answered Edwin. "Park in the spot next to hers."

Weston did as he was instructed. Edwin opened the laptop again. "Let me double-check the insurance website to see if her car still shows it's here."

Weston caught H.P.'s expression in the rearview mirror. "Old friend, it took us almost three hours to drive here, the guard told us that all the labs are closed, and Kate's car is empirically not parked next to us."

"I know." Edwin closed the laptop.

"So where does it say her car is now?" asked H.P.

"It doesn't…according to the most recent update, the device has been disconnected."

"Well, that's troubling," said Weston. "So what do you want to do?"

"H.P., would you give me the small spray bottle in the side pocket of my backpack?" asked Edwin.

H.P. handed over the plastic bottle. "What's in it?"

"Luminol."

"What the hell is luminol?" asked Weston.

"A compound that exhibits chemiluminescence," answered Edwin.

"It can detect trace amounts of blood in the dark by turning it bright blue," added H.P. "The Pirate Hunter uses it from time to time."

Weston turned to Edwin. "Follow-up question: what the hell are you doing with it?"

"I used it to track the coyotes that dragged off the chickens from their run I built out at the telescope, although it didn't really work that well since it only led me to where the coyotes ate the chickens—not to where their den was located."

"You bought luminol to track coyotes?" asked H.P.

"No, I made it. It's a relatively simple two-step process. First, I heated hydrazine in glycerol, then—"

"You kept chickens at your telescope?" interrupted Weston. "But you're a vegetarian."

"Chickens make great pets, and I enjoyed their company, though sadly the chickens' sojourn at my telescope was short-lived."

"Ed, you're a true Renaissance man," said H.P.

"What he means by that is most people haven't raised their own chickens since the Renaissance." Weston pointed to the spray bottle in Edwin's hand. "So what are you going to do with that?"

"I'm going to hope it doesn't reveal anything." Edwin exited the car and crouched over the area at the rear of Kate's empty parking spot. Weston and H.P. stood behind Edwin while he sprayed the asphalt several times. As the fine mist settled onto the blacktop, it revealed glowing blue specks on the ground.

Edwin walked slowly backwards between Weston's car and the empty parking space, spraying as he went. The three followed the trail of illuminated blue flecks up the sidewalk to the locked front door of the building.

Weston placed a hand on Edwin's shoulder. "I'm sorry I ever doubted your hunch."

Chapter 8

Weston signaled to the waitress of the all-night diner that he and his tablemates were ready for another round of coffee.

"It's nice to have customers my own age in this late." The waitress refilled Weston's mug first, then topped off H.P.'s and Edwin's. "This time of night, it's mostly college students—studying quietly during the week then drunk and loud come the weekend."

"Looks like a pretty thin crowd tonight," observed Edwin.

"Not in your case, sugar. Can I get you boys some pie to go with that coffee?"

"Thanks just the same," H.P. said, "but we're not in a dessert mood at the moment."

"Suit yourself. I'll check back in a little bit to see if you all've found your appetite."

"So should we call the cops?" asked H.P. once the waitress had left.

"We can call them," replied Weston, "though without evidence they won't do much until she's been missing for 24 hours."

"But we do have evidence—Edwin's luminol."

"Homemade luminol," said Edwin, "which I imagine would make me—and my associates—out to be crackpots in the eyes of the police. Besides, I suspect if they sprayed that whole parking lot, they'd find all kinds of bright-blue areas…that stuff is more useful on trails rarely traveled or indoors on surfaces that are frequently cleaned."

"That 24-hour thing is a stupid regulation." H.P. took a sip of coffee.

Weston nodded. "Maybe, but without it the police would spend all their time tracking down husbands who stopped off for one drink too many after work or wives who lingered a little too long at the hair salon."

H.P. set down his mug. "Okay, the guard at the gatehouse told us that he'd just come on duty before we arrived and hadn't seen anyone leave, but maybe we can call the guard who was on duty before him to ask if he saw someone else driving Kate's car."

"No, the second-shift guard got married over the weekend and is now on his honeymoon," said Edwin. "His substitute wouldn't know Kate's car by sight yet…or Kate for that matter."

Weston stirred some cream into his coffee. "A high-security place like that must have video cameras all over…would the guard in the gatehouse have access to them?"

"Nope, just the security director—who mostly works during standard business hours," answered Edwin. "But I've been thinking about that. It seems improbable that anyone could've climbed that perimeter fence without setting off an alarm of some sort…and they likely would've been spotted waiting around in the parking lot for Kate to leave, so they may've had access to the building and perhaps even her lab. If that's so, then they might've also had access to the surveillance system and could've taken the cameras offline when they abducted her."

H.P. shook his head. "Jesus Ed, I don't know if your imagination is running wild because you're worried about Kate, or if what you're saying actually makes sense, in which case this whole situation seems hopeless. I mean, if her work's security can't help us and the cops can't help us, then who can?"

"Not the cops—at least not yet," Weston replied, "but maybe one cop."

Chapter 9

Weston's cellphone chimed from the cupholder as he drove toward Chicago proper. He handed the phone to Edwin. "Can you read the text? The traffic has started to get congested now that we're getting close to the city."

"Back when I lived here, the morning rush didn't start until the sun actually came up," H.P. said from the backseat.

Edwin read the screen. "Slim texted: 'IDiOT friend found another hit on Kate license#—Canal Street exit. He'll keep searching but it'll take longer to track plate through city street camera network.' Impressive, including spaces, he used exactly 160 characters."

"The exit for Canal Street isn't too far from here," Weston said. "Any idea where we should go then?"

"Only about a thousand possibilities spring to mind," answered H.P.

"How about you, Ed?"

Edwin turned to Weston. "The only thing that makes sense to me is Union Station. She mentioned she was going there in the last email she sent. If her abductors had access to her lab, then it stands to reason they might also have been able to access her computer."

"Why would they take her there?" asked H.P.

"I don't know why, but it's the best guess I've got, so it's either that or we start dragging the river."

Weston shook his head. "Union Station doesn't open for another couple of hours."

"The station won't be open, but the parking garage will be," replied Edwin.

Weston merged into the exit lane. "We'll start there then."

****

Weston drove up the spiraling ramps of the garage as Edwin and H.P. scanned the parked cars.

"We're nearly to the top," H.P. said, "and we haven't seen any vehicle fitting your description of Kate's car."

"The lot is mostly empty," added Weston, "so I doubt we missed it either."

"Just keep going," said Edwin.

"Sure, then we can look again on the way back down to doublecheck." Weston abruptly swerved as an oversized, black SUV squealed its tires while descending the ramp in the opposite direction. "Excuse you, Excess-You-Be." Weston drove up the final ramp to the garage's roof where a single car was parked.

"That's it!" exclaimed Edwin. "That's her car."

Weston pulled into the spot next to it, and Edwin exited the car before it was fully in park. He quickly sprayed luminol around the trunk to reveal specks of blue on the bumper.

Weston looked over Edwin's shoulder. "Do you think she's still in there?"

Edwin pounded on the trunk lid. "Kate. Kate!"

As the two waited for a response, H.P. walked to the edge of the parking structure and looked down.

"No answer," said Weston. "They must've taken her someplace else."

37

"I hate to say this," H.P. replied, "but just because she didn't answer doesn't mean she isn't in there."

Weston glanced at Edwin. "Hang on, I have a tire iron in the car." Weston popped his trunk and retrieved a lug wrench with a crowbar tip. "I think I can jimmy the trunk open with this."

H.P. rejoined the other two at the rear of the car. "No, I don't think you can, but I have some experience with getting locked trunks open, so give me the lever."

Weston handed over the lug wrench. H.P. walked to the front of Kate's car and smashed the driver's side window with the wrench. He reached through the broken glass, unlocked the door, and then pushed the trunk release button on the console.

The trunk lid popped up slightly. With trepidation, Edwin slowly raised it. He let out a long sigh, both relieved and disappointed that the trunk was empty. He sprayed the floor of the trunk's interior with luminol.

The words *ON TRAIN* illumined in blue.

****

H.P. shouted at the nightwatchman through a glass door of Union Station. "We have to get inside. We think there might be someone trapped on one of your trains."

The watchman approached the door. "We don't open for another hour yet, and commuter trains don't start running until an hour after that."

"She's not a commuter. I think she might be aboard one of your trains in the railyard."

"There's just one train going anywhere right now, and the only people on it are the engineer and the cargo conductor. It's a special freight run full of lab equipment headed downstate to the university."

"We have to check it before it leaves," said H.P.

"Impossible, it's already left. It just pulled out of the station a few minutes ago after the conductor climbed aboard with a steamer trunk covered in hazmat placards—told me to stand back, if I valued my health."

"Is there any way to call it back?"

"No way that I know of," answered the watchman. "Once the Milwaukee Express clears the line, she'll be off and running."

"An express?"

"Yeah, the southbound Milwaukee Express always runs by here this time of night. Your freight train's probably stopped on the track near the river crossing, waiting for it to pass."

"Thanks, you've been most helpful." H.P. ran to Weston's waiting car and jumped into the backseat. "The only train running is a freight train that's probably waiting on the track down at the river crossing."

Weston sped away in the direction of the crossing. "Any reason to believe Kate's onboard?"

"The cargo conductor climbed aboard with a steamer trunk—apparently a last-minute addition of some hazardous lab equipment destined for the university."

"One doesn't just throw hazardous materials onto a train as it pulls out of the station," said Edwin. "There are procedures for such things."

Weston pointed in the direction of the bridge. "There's our train."

"And there goes the Milwaukee Express on the other side of the river," replied H.P.

The three watched as the silver streak blasted past, cutting a sliver through the gloom of night.

Weston accelerated. "Our train's on the move, but I think I can get us there before it crosses the river." Weston adroitly steered his car over the unreliable service road, overtaking the train as it lumbered toward the bridge. He skidded to a stop just at the river's bank and slammed his car into park. "We're going to have to make a run for it."

The three bolted out of the sedan and sprinted toward the bridge as fast as their fifty-year-old legs could carry them, catching the last railway car at the water's edge. Weston and H.P. helped Edwin climb aboard the open corridor connection on the rear of the car.

"Okay, we made it," said H.P. "Now what?"

"Let's go inside." Weston tried the latch on the door, but it was locked.

Edwin struggled to catch his breath. "On…train. She wrote…'on train'…not…'in train.'"

H.P. shook his head. "Ed, that's just a figure of speech—everyone says they're on a train even though they ride inside."

Edwin pointed to the short ladder leading up to the roof of the car. "She's…very…metic…"

"Meticulous," said Weston. "So you've mentioned."

H.P. climbed the ladder first, followed by Weston, and then Edwin.

The train picked up speed, outpacing the current of the dark river below.

"Soon we'll be out into farmland," H.P. said over the bitter wind. "What are we looking for exactly?"

Edwin espied a trunk resting atop the roof of the third car ahead. "That."

The three ran as best they could, hunched over as they were to lower their centers of gravity to keep from falling off the juddering train. H.P. leapt across to the next car, followed by Weston. Lastly, Edwin jumped but just missed the roof of the car ahead and fell into the corridor connection between. As H.P. continued on, Weston turned and looked at Edwin below. "Are you okay?"

"I think I sprained my wrist."

"Do you want me to climb down and help you up?"

"No," Edwin shouted over the clatter of the train. "I want you to keep going and help Kate."

Weston ran to catch up to H.P., who had just jumped to the car upon which the steamer trunk rested precariously.

As the train rounded a bend in the track, the trunk slid across the corrugated roof. H.P. rushed to catch it, diving for the dropdown handle on the trunk's end. He gripped the handle in one hand and a shallow ridge of the roof with his other. He heard kicking from within the trunk as the other end slid toward the edge of the roof. "I can't hold this much longer!"

Weston reached H.P. and crouched beside him, extending his arm to grab for the handle on the other end of the trunk. Like H.P., he held onto a ridge of the corrugated roof as he stretched out his hand to grasp the trunk. Finally, he grabbed hold of the handle and stopped the trunk from sliding any farther.

"We've got you," Weston shouted.

"But how do we get her out?" H.P. asked quietly. "Neither of us has a free hand."

"I can help with that." Edwin appeared behind H.P. and Weston. He crawled between their outstretched arms. "I'm here, Kate!" Edwin pulled the chain pin from the trunk's hasp fastener and flung open the lid. Kate reached out her tied hands for him, and he grasped them firmly, pulling her out onto the roof of the train.

Weston and H.P. let go of the handles and watched with exhaustion as the trunk slid off the roof and fell onto the embankment below, breaking into pieces upon impact.

"This train's really taking on speed now," said H.P. "We'd better get back down to the gangway connection before we all get blown off the roof."

Weston steadied Edwin, who was now holding his wrist, while H.P. helped Kate back to the ladder. The four managed to climb down into the small area between the two train cars. As H.P. untied Kate's hands, Weston took his cellphone from his pocket. "Slim, can you call your IDOT contact and tell him the train that just left Union Station has four stowaways on it?"

Chapter 10

Edwin, his wrist wrapped in a compression bandage, sat next to Kate, across the small table from H.P. and Weston in the interrogation room.

"I can't tell if we've been in here for an hour or a day," said Weston. "How much longer do you think they're going to keep us?"

Without raising his head from the table, H.P. answered, "I'd wager that they'll decide to cut us loose the moment I fall asleep, which I anticipate will be any minute now."

The door opened and Slim stepped into the little room. "Sorry, I could've been here sooner if they hadn't shut down Meigs Field all them years ago."

"I'm glad to see you, young man," said Edwin.

"You too, though I'm sorry to see that you got a busted wing."

"A small price to pay for the rescue of my songbird."

"10-4," Slim replied. "You boys are heroes in my book, though it took some persuading for the railroad police to see it that way. So what have they told y'all?"

H.P. rubbed his eyes. "Nothing yet."

"They took our statements and then stuck us in here," Kate added.

"What have they told you?" asked Weston.

"They're still trying to piece this thing together, but

they found the real cargo conductor stripped to his skivvies and tied up behind a dumpster in an alley a few blocks away from the station. The nightwatchman never batted an eye at not recognizing the conductor, since it was a one-off run, and the engineer only talked with the impostor through the train's intercom. It seems likely that he detrained somewhere in the railyard after toting that trunk up to the roof. Miss, you didn't happen to get a good look at him, didja?"

"No," answered Kate. "They blindfolded me at my lab, so I didn't really see either of them, but I heard them talking, while I suppose they were waiting in the parking garage for the conductor to show up for work—that is, before they transferred me from my car trunk to that steamer trunk. That's how I knew to write 'ON TRAIN' in blood inside my trunk."

"They didn't hurt you, did they?" asked Slim.

"No, not really. I was only bleeding because I slipped off my shoes and was literally dragging my feet as they carried me to my car so that Eddie might find my trail with the homemade luminol that he inexplicably has with him at all times."

"If not for my luminol, you—"

Kate put a finger to his mouth. "It's okay, Eddie…I love that you're eccentric."

"What I still don't understand is why this plan was so damn dumb," said Weston. "I mean why go to all the trouble to kidnap Kate, then put her on top of a train only to leave her there. Why not just shoot her and throw her body in the river—no offense, Kate—or if these morons have a thing for trains, then why not tie her to the tracks like Snidely Whiplash might've done?"

Kate grinned. "Actually, when they were deciding

how to respond to Eddie's call from your phone to mine, I heard them make that same reference."

"Ah, learned men," replied Weston.

H.P. yawned. "I've been thinking about their cockamamie plan too, and really it's rather ingenious."

Weston raised his hands toward H.P. "Please enlighten us, oh wise one."

"I'd be glad to. Edwin mentioned that the assailants may've had access to Kate's work computer, from which she sent the email about her going to Union Station. If so, then they might've been trying to make her disappearance look like a suicide. After all, they drove her car to Union Station, rather than just putting her in the back of their SUV. Then they put her on a train traveling the same line as the train she should've been on earlier, since it wouldn't have looked like a very convincing suicide had her body been found in the train yard where the trains move slowly. The conductor couldn't have thrown her from the train himself when it was moving fast, since there'd be no way for him to then get off the train until reaching its destination, at which point the ruse might have been discovered. They didn't drug Kate, which would've made things simpler, since an unconscious person is easier to handle than one who can thrash about—opting instead to Taser her—so that no suspicious chemicals would be found in her system during an autopsy. As for the trunk, I imagine they figured—probably quite accurately—that it would not slide off the roof until the train was moving fast enough that a fall wouldn't have been survivable. You saw how that trunk broke apart when it landed. If Kate had been inside it, the trunk would've disintegrated around her, appearing merely as railway detritus rather than the means of her confinement. Moreover, the train likely wouldn't have reached sufficient velocity to fling the trunk from its roof until it was in an unpopulated area, thus delaying her discovery and making any evidence of foul play that much more difficult to ascertain."

"That's an inventive theory," said Weston, "but they knew the actual conductor would eventually be found or else declared missing."

H.P. nodded. "Yes, one way or another, their subterfuge was destined to be exposed, but I have no doubt that they were aware of that. In fact, I suspect if the cargo aboard that train is tallied against the manifest, it'll be discovered that an item or two is missing, making the whole scheme—if it had gone off without a hitch—seem like a train robbery rather than a homicide by rail."

Slim smiled. "That's a pretty clever deduction, H.P. I see now why you don't waste your talent writing romance novels like Weston. A small case is missing."

"A case?" asked Kate. "What did it contain?"

"Miscellaneous chemicals," answered Slim. "The manifest didn't specify any more than that. Okay, you four sit tight a little longer. The railroad detectives are taking the conductor's statement now, so once they're done with him, they'll probably have a few more questions for you and then let you all go."

Chapter 11

Weston drove the empty stretch of interstate between Chicago and home, attempting every few minutes to tune in a radio station that was broadcasting something other than a morning farm report or country music.

"You might as well give it up and put in a CD," said H.P. from the passenger's seat.

"The search keeps me awake."

"Why don't you pull into the next gas station and get some coffee?"

"Because then twenty minutes later I'd have to pull off again to get rid of the coffee."

"Then why don't you let me drive for a while?"

"You've been nodding off for the past hour," Weston said.

"Which means I've had more sleep than you."

"I'm fine. I just want to get home."

"Yeah, me too. Do you remember when crazy nights out used to be fun, and the last thing you wanted to do was go home?"

"Barely." Weston turned off the radio. "A thought occurred to me while you were kipping."

"What, that 'kipping' is a silly synonym for 'sleeping'?"

"No, I was mulling over your theory about Kate's kidnapping."

"See, wouldn't 'kidnapping' make more sense as a synonym for sleeping, putting one in mind as it does of the phrase 'sleeping like a baby'?"

"Take it from someone who has a baby at home, they don't sleep all that well. May I get back to my line of thinking now?"

H.P. watched out the window as they drove past a long, frost covered field. "By all means."

"The more I thought about it, the more I think her abductors might've already had the train heist planned, and that Kate's abduction was a last-minute addendum of sorts to their plan—kind of a two-birds-with-one-stone scenario."

"So you think someone instructed the kippers to swing by Kate's lab on their way to Union Station, making it a 'take an item, leave an item' type of proposition?"

"Can we not do a whole drawn out thing with kippers?" asked Weston. "It's late…or rather it's early. Either way I'm exhausted, so congratulations—you had some fun with wordplay. Let's move on…what do you say?"

"Sure, we can skip the whole kip and caboodle."

Weston inhaled deeply through his nose and then let out an exaggerated breath. "But what about the purloined case? Do you think its theft was premeditated?"

"Do I think the ersatz conductor who was really an abductor premeditated the purloining of the case instead of simply meditating its purloinment in the moment?"

"I mentioned the part about me being exhausted, didn't I?"

H.P. tried to open his eyes wide. "Sorry, I must be

a little punchy myself. What you're suggesting isn't impossible, of course, but from what little description Slim gave us, it didn't sound as if the contents of the case were any great shakes."

"Right, 'miscellaneous chemicals' The more I turned that phrase over in my head the more it transitioned from generic to cryptic."

"So what sorts of chemicals do you think could've been in the case?" asked H.P.

"Well, a chemical is either a gas like a chemical weapon, such as mustard gas, or a liquid…say for instance, hydrochloric acid, right?"

"No, I think a chemical can be a solid too…like what you use to put out a chemical fire."

"You mean like a flame retardant?" asked Weston. "That's a liquid too when it's inside the fire extinguisher."

"Right, but it becomes a solid when it's introduced to air—like whipped cream from a can."

"Whipped cream isn't a solid."

"Can you drink it?"

Weston nodded. "When it melts you can."

"You could drink anything when it melts."

"You couldn't drink my car."

"If you melted it down to molten metal you could—at least until it killed you."

"So then a chemical can be a gas, liquid, or a solid?" Weston asked.

"Do you sometimes get the feeling that we're not as smart as we think we are?"

Chapter 12

Edwin and Kate cautiously entered her condo. Kate quickly deadbolted the door behind them and then went from room to room, turning on all the lights.

"Are you sure you wouldn't feel safer at a hotel?" asked Edwin. "If they know where you work then they surely know where you live."

Kate entered the living room from the brightly lit bedroom. "You think I don't know that? But I refuse to live in fear."

"Well, it's going to be difficult to sleep in there with the lights on."

"I'm too afraid to sleep." Kate reentered the kitchen. "Care for a beer, Eddie?"

Edwin took a seat on the couch. "Not particularly."

"Turning down a free beer—you must be a little scared yourself."

"Hell, yes I am. I almost lost you. You know, there's nothing wrong with refusing to live in fear while living in hiding."

Kate returned from the kitchen with a glass of wine and sat next to Edwin. "But this is my home."

"Let's put that in abeyance for a moment. So what do you think this was all about? I got the sense that you weren't telling the police everything you know."

"I told them everything I know to be a fact, but I don't believe their investigation would've benefited from me sharing my highly speculative suppositions."

"You seemed awfully curious about the contents of that missing case," said Edwin. "Frankly, I was too, with a description as vague and all-encompassing as 'miscellaneous chemicals.' Unless a case happens to contain a perfect vacuum, the contents of every case in existence could be described as containing miscellaneous chemicals."

"True," Kate replied, "but everything about the train seemed wrong."

"How so? The railroad detective's explanation that the university didn't want their fragile and newly donated lab equipment mixed in with all the cargo on a conventional freight train and run the risk of some of it being damaged or misrouted seemed sufficiently plausible."

"Sufficient perhaps, but not satisfactory—at least not for me. A train that size could've carried enough equipment for a dozen labs. Did the university recently build such a facility?"

"As far as I know, there aren't any new science facilities on campus," Edwin answered. "So you don't think that equipment was intended for the university?"

"I imagine some of it was, but it wouldn't surprise me that for every two pieces of equipment that goes in the front door, one will go out the back. I've heard of it happening before; it's a good way to launder lab equipment, so to speak."

Edwin shook his head. "I don't think the university would be party to something like that."

"Probably not wittingly but possibly as part of the deal with whoever funded the donation of all that new equipment. Maybe they agreed to take the old equipment off the university's hands, perhaps offering a vague assurance to in turn donate it to some other less-fortunate institution. The university would get the latest and shiniest toys to show off, while whoever would get loads of secondhand lab equipment without any of the documentation that comes from making a direct purchase of that size for a private entity. A Bunsen burner still makes a flame no matter if it's thirty years old or fresh from the box."

"Okay, that's interesting…and disturbing, but it still doesn't offer any clues about the actual contents of the case."

"Maybe whatever is in the case was the one thing that whoever these potentially nefarious benefactors are didn't want to take the chance of getting lost in the shuffle, perhaps by some overcurious grad student opening it upon arrival and pilfering its contents. After all, if you ordered a case of diamonds, you'd have them shipped to you in an armored truck, but if you ordered a case of priceless diamonds, then you might think it wiser to have the case labeled carbon compounds and shipped with a bunch of other similar-looking cargo, hoping no one would notice until you had an opportunity to retrieve them for yourself."

"That's so devious," said Edwin.

"Smuggling is a devious business."

"No, I meant that you thought that whole scheme up based on what the detective told us."

"Eddie, it's just a working hypothesis…maybe I'm connecting dots that don't actually go together."

"Not to worry. Weston does that all the time, and even when he's wrong, he frequently manages to stumble onto something intriguing. So what's your best guess as to what these priceless diamonds really are?"

"Speaking of stumbling onto something intriguing, remember me telling you about that sub-rosa project I discovered at work? I think they're further along than I initially realized."

Edwin stared up at the ceiling for a moment. "Perhaps I will have that beer."

Chapter 13

Weston descended the stairs in his pajamas and found Becky and the kids at the dining room table eating pizza.

"Care to join us for breakfast?" asked Becky.

"This is dinner, not breakfast," said Lance.

Weston sat down and took a slice from the box. "Not for me, buddy."

"All-nighter, huh?" Van shook his head. "By the looks of you, it was a rough one."

"You don't know the half of it," replied Weston. "Used to be I could skip a night of sleep and still function, now, if I stay up all night I have to sleep all day, but—in one of those ironies of growing old—I often have trouble sleeping through the night."

"Maybe you're turning into a vampire," offered Lance.

"That might not be so bad," said Weston. "I'd prefer to see no reflection in the mirror rather than the old man staring back at me these days."

"Well old-timer, if you hadn't gotten up soon, I was going to wake you." Becky wiped tomato sauce from Ance's face. "Company is on the way. Seems your friends can't go a day without seeing you."

"Why didn't you tell them that I've taken gravely ill and am not to be disturbed?"

"H.P. and Ed are coming in from out of town to see

you," answered Becky. "It sounded important."

"I wonder whose life I'm going to have to save tonight."

"You saved somebody's life last night?" asked Van.

"Yes, but it was a team effort...though I did all the driving."

****

"I suppose I'm driving again," said Weston as he exited the house with Edwin and H.P.

"Actually, I'll drive tonight," replied Edwin, "since I know where we're going."

Weston watched as Edwin pulled a key fob from his pocket. "You don't even have a car."

"That's true, but I borrowed Kate's and she in turn borrowed H.P.'s."

"It's a good deal for me," said H.P. "In exchange for my beater, I get a chauffeur who drives a luxury car...kind of like yours Weston, but newer."

Weston eyed the expensive sedan with a plastic-covered driver's side window at the end of the driveway. "I thought Kate was supposed to be smart. Why would she make such a dumb trade?"

"We drove down to H.P.'s place this afternoon," answered Edwin. "Then she switched cars, both because no one will know to look for her in H.P.'s car or search for its license plate and because it lacks all the very trackable electronic accoutrements of her high-tech vehicle. She's driving down south to stay with an old college roommate. Even I don't know exactly where she's going."

"That makes sense," said Weston. "If she wasn't safe at work, then she wouldn't have been safe at home either."

The sedan started up as Edwin opened the driver's side door. "I quite agree, though it took some convincing for her to see it that way, but when the police dropped off her car earlier today after the evidence-recovery team finished their search, they confirmed that the surveillance cameras around her lab at the time of her abduction had been offline, so she knew she was no longer safe in or around the city."

Weston bumped into H.P. as they both reached for the passenger side's door handle. "I'm accustomed to riding up front."

"But I already adjusted the seat to my liking," H.P. replied.

"I suppose that's the middle-aged version of calling shotgun."

Chapter 14

Weston leaned forward from the backseat to talk with the occupants of the front seats. "So where are we going?"

Edwin glanced in the rearview mirror. "What are you going to ask next—are we there yet?"

"Sitting back here, I do feel rather like a child, though the smart-alecky kids I usually drive around ask 'Are we there yet?' before they even get in the car."

"Does Ance's car seat even fit in your backseat?" asked H.P.

"It fits fine, but my car predates the LATCH system, and it takes about an hour to thread the seat belt through the damn thing, so we don't usually bother, which is okay with me since I'm not too keen on getting Cheerios and toddler slobber on my leather upholstery."

"You could always get rid of it," H.P. suggested.

"I'm not going to get rid of my baby."

"I won't bother asking if your response was intended to be figurative or literal," said Edwin.

"You could bother answering my question."

"We're going to a round barn that's been temporarily converted into a covert pool hall. A former classmate from grad school, who previously did contract work for a chemistry concern that sometimes partners on projects with Kate's company, is playing in an itinerant pool league there; he's one of several sharps who participates in this peripatetic circuit. The pros shoot a few games against each other; wagers are made—money won and lost as the rankings are posted online. Afterwards, locals have an opportunity to play against the best, often losing small fortunes for the privilege of doing so."

"How is this in my own backyard, and I've never heard of it?" asked Weston.

"And if these guys are so great, then why are they playing in a barn and not some big venue in the city?" H.P. added.

"From what I understand, most of this league's players make more than they would on the pro tour, but then their earnings aren't exactly aboveboard. Small towns are a good place to keep something a secret. Besides, rural localities offer the two things a pool circuit like this thrives on—fast-traveling word of mouth and a dearth of entertainment options. Each night, the tournament packs up and continues on to the next town, before the area's constabulary gets wise and raids their gambling operation."

"So why are H.P. and I tagging along to see this pool-playing professor?"

"Because if we're to figure out who's behind Kate's abduction—"

"Pardon me," H.P. interrupted, "but is that what we're doing?"

"Yes…isn't that the type of thing you two do these days?"

"It is indeed," Weston confirmed.

"Then I thought it a good idea to seek out the counsel of a polymath…possibly the most intelligent person I know."

Weston cleared his throat. "Of course, present company excluded."

H.P. shook his head. "Deluded and included, I think is more accurate."

"Oh," said Edwin, "another thing—despite the university issuing him PhDs like parking tickets as a young man, he's not a professor."

"How come?" H.P. asked. "Does he have a gambling issue?"

"Hardly…his issue is more esoteric in nature."

"That's the pot calling the kettle metal," said Weston. "What's his problem then?"

"He has a tic. He's called Hooper because he makes a distinctive hooping noise each time he has a thought or, as you'll likely see this evening, takes a shot, making him something of a colorful character on the clandestine pool circuit, but precluding him from a professorship at an institution befitting his intellect."

"And what makes him so smart?" asked Weston.

"For starters, he can solve a three-body problem in his head."

"I'm certain I'd be impressed if I knew what that was," said H.P.

"You know, spherical cows."

H.P. nodded. "Of course, Ed, why didn't you say so?"

"So we're off to brainstorm with a barnstormer at a billiards barn burner." Weston leaned back. "As it happens, the last time H.P. and I were in a barn together, it actually burned to the ground."

Chapter 15

Weston, Edwin, and H.P. approached the round barn from the frozen cornfield-cum-parking lot. Edwin eyed the door. "Just as I suspected—they're using a judas hole."

"Better than a glory hole, I suppose," said Weston.

As the trio neared the entrance, the slat inset in the steel door slid open to reveal a stern set of eyes. "Who are you here to see?"

"Hooper," Edwin answered.

"You follow his stats, do you?"

"I wouldn't be here to see him in person if I didn't."

"Not counting tonight's wins, how many of his last 15 matches has he won?"

"Seven."

"What's that make his winning percentage then?"

"Four hundred followed by more sixes than you can count," answered Edwin.

The slat shut and the door opened. A man of imposing stature held the door for them as they entered.

Weston looked the man up and down. "You must have to do a lot of crouching to stay at eye level."

"I sit on a stool," the tall man replied.

The trio walked into the large, open space. Several pool tables occupied the center of the barn—most with cash stacked up on the rails. A cacophony of squabbling and coarse language filled the air.

Edwin motioned to the bar. "This isn't my scene, so I'm going to go get a drink and maybe stuff shredded bits of napkins in my ears."

"Wait, aren't you going to introduce us to your friend?" asked H.P.

"I never said we were friends. Actually, it'd probably be better if you didn't mention my name. I just came along to get you in the door. Tell him what you know about Kate's situation and see what he thinks."

"Can you at least point him out to us?" Weston asked.

"Sure, he's over in the corner."

Weston started to scan the circular room and then smiled. "Cute."

"I told you why they call him Hooper. He won't be hard to find, but I'm going to make myself scarce before he spots me."

Weston and H.P. circled the tables as Edwin veered off for the bar. The clamor around the far table was particularly loud.

A young man in a garish green suit tucked a hundred-dollar bill under the rail cushion nearest him and then rolled the cue ball to the opposite end of the otherwise empty table.

A man with a gray ponytail rose from a chair and approached the table. "Five rails?"

The young man nodded. "That's right, old-timer. You bank that cue ball off five rails and get it to land down here on Mr. Benjamin, then he's all yours, but if the bank is closed and you miss, then you owe me a hundo."

The bespectacled man studied the cue ball for a moment and the placement of the bill at the far end of the table. Then he stretched out his pool cue in front of him, making a closed bridge on the table's felt, and carefully took aim at an area near the side pocket. He slowly pulled back the cue and then rapidly propelled it forward, letting out a "hoop" that could've been mistaken for a rebel yell. The cue ball swiftly bounced off one cushion and then another, zigzagging across the table until it finally lost momentum after hitting the fifth cushion, and came to rest on the hundred-dollar bill.

"Nice shot, old man."

"The man on the money is old." The ponytailed sharp stood up straight. "I'm only middle-aged. Want to go for double or nothing?"

The young man took a step back into the crowd around the table. "Nah, I'm good."

"Anyone else then?" The man wiped the lenses of his glasses on his untucked aloha shirt as he waited for takers. "Put a C-note along any rail you want, and I'll make the cue ball stop on it after hitting five rails."

Weston stepped forward. "Are you Hooper?"

The man frowned. "Yes, though people don't usually call me that to my face."

"That was an impressive trick shot, but I don't want to make a wager. I only need a moment of your time to ask you a question."

"Time is money, and I'm working."

Weston shook his head. "Uh, I don't think I have a C-note on me, but my friend H.P. might."

"A hundred, huh?" asked H.P.

The ponytailed man nodded.

"What if I can make the shot instead…get the cue ball to stop on the hundred dollars. Will you answer our question then?"

"It's not as easy as I make it look."

Weston grabbed H.P.'s arm as he approached the table. "You sure you know what you're doing? Last time we played pool, I beat you soundly, and I'm horrible."

H.P. pulled his wallet from his sport coat and then folded the coat over Weston's outstretched arm. "I happen to know a tricky shot myself, but thanks for the vote of confidence." He opened his wallet and dropped more than a dozen bills on the playing field—two twenties, three tens, a few fives, and some ones. H.P. quickly spread out the money on the felt, imbricating the edges of the bills so they papered a path from siderail to siderail.

The ponytailed man grinned. "That's clever, but you still have to make the shot—five rails."

A man standing in the crowd gathered around the table handed H.P. a cue stick. H.P. set the cue ball in the middle of the greenback pathway and took aim at the rail directly across from him. "I'm terrible at this game…the only thing I know how to do well is shoot straight." The cue ball shot forward, hit the rail and bounced directly back; H.P. immediately moved his pool cue off the table so as not to obstruct the ball's return. The cue ball hit off rails thrice more before slowing to a crawl near the side pocket and gently impacting a rail for the fifth time, finally coming to a rest a fraction of an inch from the edge of a one-dollar bill.

The crowd looked to the ponytailed man for a

reaction.

"You're a straight shooter all right." Hooper grinned again. "What your shot lacked in skill, it made up for in style—well played."

H.P. handed back the cue stick and collected his money off the table. "Thanks...now about that question."

"Sure, but let's talk over there and give the table a chance to cool for a bit." H.P. and Weston followed Hooper to a less crowded area away from the pool tables. "I admit that you've piqued my curiosity—*hoop*. What is it that you two are so desperate to know?"

"First of all," H.P. said, "what's a three-body problem and what the hell does it have to do with spherical cows?"

"Ah, yes—*hoop*—a three-body problem is calculating how three bodies in space will influence each other's velocity and motion...think pool balls—or spherical cows, if you like. Shooting a combination shot is the easiest thing in the world—just keep one eye on the cue ball, the other on the object ball, and another on the ball it'll hit. That's a three-body problem, except of course a pool table only has two dimensions while space has that tricky third one."

"So why does a physicist go into chemistry?" asked Weston. "We understand that you used to work for a chemical concern that is frankly of concern to us."

"I am something of a factotum, and in fact chemical engineer was one of my many occupations, be it ever so brief."

"A friend of ours was kidnapped yesterday from her lab at [company name redacted]," said Weston. "We were told your former employer had a partnership with her company, and we think whatever they were developing together could be the reason for her attempted abduction."

"Attempted?" Hooper asked. "I take it then that Kate's okay now?"

H.P. glanced at Weston. "How did you—"

"I see Edwin trying to look invisible over there by the bar—*hoop*. I'm still in contact with some of my university friends, and I heard they were together. He must think I'm still sore about losing the privilege of staying in that rundown radio telescope all those years ago."

"Yes, Kate is fine now," Weston said. "And if it makes you feel any better, that telescope was blown to bits a few months back."

"Yeah, I heard that too…*hoop*. A real shame…it was a beauty back in its day. So you two are clearly chasing after something, but what are you hoping to catch?"

"The bad guys, of course," answered Weston. "But for starters we'd settle for a motive…was what they were working on worth killing for?"

"I can't say what specifically Kate's company or mine were working on. I wasn't at my job long enough to be entrusted with any of the real hush-hush projects, but certainly there were rumors—from genetically modifying corn in unseemly ways to creating next-level hallucinogens. Contrary to conventional thinking, chemistry is not an exact science. So many chemical breakthroughs over the past century have been due to mad scientists—*hoop*—just tinkering…pet projects to test if they could do something before anybody bothered to ask whether they should. Take polytetrafluorethylene for example, you know, Teflon—first used in the development of the atomic bomb, then to coat pots and pans, now it's on the naughty-forever chemicals list. Only tomorrow can tell if today's new chemistry concoctions will help or harm humanity, so these scientists like to keep their experiments a secret—ironically, sometimes by partnering with other labs so that techs in either don't fully understand the scope of a given project they're collaborating on."

H.P. sighed. "So despite being potentially awful, these partnerships aren't unique."

"That's about the size of it—*hoop*. I knew Kate by reputation, but I never worked with her directly, though I did collaborate virtually with her team for a time on a CRISPR project to edit mosquito DNA. The idea was to reengineer mosquitos using subviral RNA-agents so that rather than being vectors for disease they would instead inject their hosts with a biological vaccine to counteract that which their brethren—or more accurately I suppose, sistren—so often carry. The CRISPR part worked fine. The modified mosquitos reproduced naturally—generation over generation, at least in the lab—with the DNA recombination we introduced. However, the biotic inoculation proved problematic, with side effects that included vivid nightmares, profound anxiety, aggression, delusional paranoia, dissociative psychosis, and severe memory loss. So the project was scrapped, which could of course mean it was merely moved to another lab—*hoop*."

"Jesus," said Weston, "that sounds like something out of a sci-fi story that a hack writer slash creative-writing instructor at a middling Midwest university might come up with."

"More often than not, science fiction eventually ends up becoming science fact—*hoop*. Did either of you ever imagine that people would one day talk into their wristwatches like Dick Tracy?"

"How come we always get the dumb ones, but never the cool stuff like flying cars?" Weston asked rhetorically. "I've been waiting years now to trade in my car for a flying model."

"What's the meaning of that term you mentioned?" asked H.P. "Crisper, was it?"

"CRISPR is an acronym—*hoop*—stands for: Clustered Regularly Interspaced Short Palindromic Repeats."

H.P. sighed again. "I think I know what most of those words mean, but I have no idea what they all mean when you string them together like that."

Weston clucked his tongue. "Such a simpleton."

"Like I told you before…mad-scientist stuff—*hoop*—think *The Island of Doctor Moreau* but on a molecular level."

"That seems like something someone might kill for to keep secret," said Weston.

"Could be—*hoop*—though it might not—"

The sound of a steel door being forcefully separated from its hinges interrupted Hooper's statement and brought all other noises in the barn to an abrupt halt. The three turned to see a man in a brown cowboy hat enter, followed by a phalanx of police officers.

"*Hoop*. That's my cue to exit. I suggest you two do likewise. Good luck with your hunting expedition."

Weston and H.P. watched as Hooper scampered away with the retreating crowd, then they turned toward the bar to see a flummoxed Edwin being placed in handcuffs.

"I guess we'd better go help him before he freaks out," said H.P.

"He is our ride."

Chapter 16

Edwin paced anxiously behind the bars of their cell door. "I've got to get out of here."

"Ed, you're working yourself up for no reason," said Weston. "Come back and have a seat on this bench."

"I can't sit on that uncomfortable metal bench anymore…I can't stay in here any longer."

"Last night you were hanging on top of a freight car," H.P. said, "but tonight you can't sit on a bench?"

"Last night I was trying to save Kate. Tonight, I'm caged like an animal in this prison."

"I think you're being a little overdramatic, my friend." Weston stood up to stretch. "This is jail—not prison, and we've only been here an hour or so…and they were nice enough to give us our own cell."

"We even have our own commode," added H.P.

Edwin eyed the stainless-steel facilities in the corner. "It's attached to the sink—that can't be sanitary."

"I'm sure Slim will be here soon to spring us," Weston said.

H.P. put his feet up on the bench. "Let's talk about something else to get your mind off our surroundings."

"What should we talk about?" asked Edwin.

"You were okay on top of the train because you wanted to help Kate. Let's try to help her cause now by discussing what we learned from Hooper, and maybe in the process it'll help you with being okay in here."

"H.P. makes a good point." Weston leaned against the graffitied concrete wall. "Do you think what we mentioned about that CRISPR project during our paddy-wagon ride over is the motive for Kate's kidnapping?"

Edwin turned from the bars of the cell door. "No, that's not something Kate's group would've worked on, which jibes with what Hooper had to say. The CRISPR aspect of the project more likely would've been handled by his erstwhile organization. Besides, that technology is on the cusp of becoming commonplace—not something to commit murder over. I remember Kate telling me a while ago about their part in the attempted development of a vaccine for common mosquito-borne diseases—though I wasn't aware of the plans for its unconventional means of administration—but just as Hooper told you, the neurological side effects were deemed too severe, so it was abandoned."

"Then it's a dead end," said H.P.

Edwin looked up at the ceiling. "Maybe not. The mosquito angle is interesting. What if rather than editing their DNA to produce a biotic vaccine, they were instead designed to generate and deliver a different sort of payload?"

"So far, that sounds bad," Weston replied, "very bad."

"If the mosquitos were manipulated to create and carry a chemical formula Kate recently told me of her misgivings about, then it could be very bad indeed…though I can't imagine anything as bad as some of the graffiti on this ceiling. How does a limericist even get up there?"

Slim approached the other side of the cell door shaking his head. "Do you know what I like best?"

Edwin turned. "I'm glad to see you, young man."

"Ed, you said that same thing last night." Weston stood up from the wall. "Slim, couldn't you have gotten here any sooner?"

"Now don't go interrupting me," replied Slim. "I had the whole midnight drive over here to think about this. On a warm day, I like to fish with my bare feet in a cool pond, but what I like even better than that is the taste of pecan pie fresh from the oven; however, what I like best of all is a good night's sleep…especially if my sleep happened to be interrupted the night before—as it was last evening, by you three."

"Just imagine how well you'll sleep tomorrow," Weston said.

"Oh, you can count on it, because tomorrow night I'm turning off my phone and then locking it in the damn gun safe."

Chapter 17

Two men wearing dark suits sat on the couch in the waiting room with a case resting between them. The receptionist looked up again from her desk. "He's usually here by now."

"It's fine ma'am, we don't mind waiting."

"Are you sure I can't get you two some coffee…or water?"

The other man shook his head. "No thanks, ma'am."

She eyed the stack of technical journals on the coffee table. "Sorry if our magazines aren't to your liking. He typically only has meetings with scientist types. I can go out to the front lobby to see if they have any sports magazines."

"That won't be necessary, ma'am."

The other man smiled. "Ma'am, if you don't mind my asking, what makes you think we're not scientists…because he's tall and I'm short?"

"No, scientists come in all shapes and sizes, but most of them don't dress as well as you two…or call me ma'am."

A bald man hurriedly entered the reception area. "My apologies for being late—they just mentioned in the lobby that I had visitors waiting for me."

"No apology necessary, sir."

"When they told me you'd be stopping by first

thing in the morning, I was thinking more ten-ish…that's what passes for early around here. Anyway, follow me into my office." He held the door open as the two men entered with the case. "If these two gentlemen ever return, you can just let them wait in my office…and hold my calls."

"Who's going to call you this time of day?" asked the receptionist as the door to the inner office closed.

"Have a seat, you two." The anxious man sat down in the chair behind his desk and then stood up again. "Can I get you some coffee?"

"No thank you, sir."

The bald man sat down once more. "Sorry if I seem jumpy…it's just sort of surreal to actually meet you both in person. Do you two have names?"

"Yes," answered the other man.

"Well…uh, what should I call you?"

"I go by George and he's Geoff."

"Oh, I thought you'd have code names or something…I have nephews named Jeff and George."

The other man smiled. "You can call me Mr. Snide and him Mr. Whip."

"Okay—that's more like it." The bald man leaned back in his desk chair, yet somehow still looked nervous. "So have you had any luck tracking down Kate?"

"The trail has gone cold, sir," said Mr. Whip.

"We tailed her downstate yesterday," Mr. Snide said, "but we had to give her distance when she started driving through less-populated areas. We think she might've switched cars in central Illinois, since her car is now being driven by her boyfriend, one Edwin Hubert, but there's no sign of her, and so far, we haven't gotten any hits on her credit cards."

"Kate's too smart for that. You were right...as you'd suggested before, I should've let you two disappear her Jason Bourne style rather than my ad hoc *Throw Mama from the Train* gambit."

"It was an emergent situation, sir. You already had us working the one job...it wasn't a bad call to try and shoehorn this other task into that operation."

"And it's not a movie." Mr. Snide stood and set the case on the desk. "There are just too many variables to make predictions with any certainty, but we did achieve the primary objective."

The bald man sat up straight and pulled the case toward him. With trembling fingers, he flipped up its catches. A cold fog billowed out from under the lid. "Yes, I shudder to think what might've happened had this found its way into the wrong hands." He closed the case and set it under his desk. "Still, I'd rest easier if Kate didn't suspect its existence."

Mr. Whip opened his hands reassuringly. "Don't worry sir, she'll pop back up on the association's radar."

"We have associates everywhere—some embedded within law enforcement," added Mr. Snide. "We'll find her, and if not, then it means she's hidden herself so well that she's gone too far underground to cause you any trouble."

The bald man placed his elbows on the desk. "I wish I could believe that, but I suppose there's nothing that can be done now until she makes a move."

"We did discover one interesting detail," said Mr. Whip. "The target's boyfriend has been in the association's crosshairs before."

"Ed? That's surprising. I mean, I only met the guy once, but he hardly seemed like a threat…to anyone."

"He wasn't the primary target," Mr. Snide said, "but rather a friend of someone our association was contracted to eliminate by your council, though ultimately the subcommittee in charge of that particular operation had a change of heart."

"Huh." The bald man leaned back in his chair again. "Is there any chance you could squeeze him to get to Kate?"

Mr. Whip nodded. "Sure, it might be worth a try."

Chapter 18

Despite drinking his entire thermos of coffee, H.P. had barely been able to stay awake through his first class of the day. As he descended the stairs to his subterranean office in the basement of the English Building, he considered refilling his thermos and periodically splashing the hot coffee on his face to keep himself from falling asleep. A student had scheduled an appointment during his office hour before his next class, but more often than not the morning appointments turned out to be no-shows, so he thought maybe he could put his head down on his desk for forty winks. No such luck—as H.P. rounded the corner he saw his student waiting in the corridor.

"Good morning." H.P. unlocked his door and held it open for the young man to enter.

The student sat and wasted no time mincing words. "I need your advice."

H.P. took his seat languidly. "Sure, what's up?"

"I'm working on this novel about a group of androids who look just like humans, but they have superhuman abilities, and they're considered a threat to society, so they're hunted by special police officers called—"

"Blade Runners?" asked H.P.

"No…I don't know what those are. I was going to say Humanoid Hunters. Anyway, these cops have a test for identifying androids that impersonate humans."

"Wait, are you sure you've never heard of *Blade Runner*?"

The student tilted his head to the side. "Is that a book or something?"

"Well, it's a movie based on a book by Philip Dick, but it had a different title. The film starred Harrison Ford."

"Is he the inventor of the Model T?"

"Let's move on. So the Blade—er, Hunters have a test…"

"Right, they ask people to tell time on an analog clock. You see, the androids are very literal, so they can glance at a clock face for a split second and tell you exactly what time it is…say 4:46, whereas we humans would say quarter till five."

H.P. leaned forward in his chair. "Hmm, that's interesting. So what can I help you with?"

"I'm having trouble coming up with the title. I plan for the sequel to be entitled *Second Hand*, for obvious reasons, but would it make more sense for the first book to be called *Minute Hand* or *Hour Hand*…or should I maybe go in a different direction and entitle the first book *Short Hand* and the follow up *Long Hand*? But then that might put readers in mind of writing by hand rather than clocks."

"I understand your concern about the sequel title, but tell me…how far along are you in writing the first one?"

The student shook his head. "With all my schoolwork and making spring-break plans, I haven't really begun the actual writing process yet, but I thought I'd start working on it after I get back from

Cancun and then try to finish up before I leave for my summer abroad. Maybe I can bring by the first draft at the end of the semester for you to review, and you can give me some notes on it when I return from Europe."

"Notes on your unwritten novel that you intend to complete between spring break and the end of the semester?"

"Sure…maybe after you've read it, you'll have some suggestions for titling it."

"I'll certainly be around, so feel free to drop it by once it's finished."

****

H.P. stepped carefully down the staircase into the basement of the English Building, holding the handrail to steady himself. The second thermos of coffee he drank to get him through his second class of the morning had left him jittery. He felt the coffee in his stomach slosh about with each step he took, making him feel a little nauseous. His plan was to skip lunch, lock himself in his office, and take a nap before his afternoon class.

As he turned the corner, a student standing in front of his office door waved at him excitedly. "I'm so glad I caught you. I know this is probably your lunch hour, but I was wondering if you could spare a few minutes. I woke up last night after this really weird dream, and I can't get it out of my head, so I thought maybe it would be a good idea for a story, but because I didn't get much sleep, I'm not sure if my judgement is off—know what I mean?"

"Indubita—babble…without a doubt." H.P. opened his office door, and the young woman entered.

Before H.P. took his seat, the student began

explaining her idea. "Okay, so there are these two parallel worlds, but they're actually mirror realities of one another."

"Hmm, that's interesting."

"I know, right? Anyway, the people in this world have doppelgangers in the other, but they are opposites—like a smart guy here would be a dumb guy there, and a genius would be a... I don't know what the correct term—"

"Developmentally disabled?" H.P. offered.

"'Disabled' doesn't sound right, but you get what I'm saying. So there's this evil genius who takes over this world, and there's nothing that can be done about it. I mean it's like the end of days...our worst nightmare—Hitler on steroids. But this unlikely hero finds a way to breach the barrier between our world and that parallel world, and furthermore, he figures out that if he travels to that mirror reality and kills this evil genius's other self then the villain will lose like half his intelligence and be easier to defeat, giving us a chance."

"But the other world's version of this evil genius would be developmentally disabled, no?"

"Right, and again I don't think 'disabled' is the correct term, but I mean it's just one guy against the fate of all humanity in this world."

H.P. nodded. "I understand that, and don't get me wrong...it's an intriguing concept, but the thought of someone murdering a developmentally—er, cognitively-impaired person to save a reality no one in that world would know existed doesn't seem very heroic."

"Well, I did say, 'unlikely hero,' and, by the way, 'impaired' doesn't seem like the right word either...but

I see your point. What if the evil genius's doppelganger was his opposite in a different way?"

"Like how?"

"Maybe instead of evil, he was kind."

H.P. nodded again. "So the hero would travel from this world to murder the kindest person in that world?"

"Yeah…another good point." The young woman gazed at him for a moment. "What if the evil genius was left-handed…and his doppelganger was a righty?"

"Sure, I don't think anybody would get too bent out of shape about that."

****

Having finished his third and final class of the day, H.P. considered just falling to the floor and rolling himself down the stairs to the basement of the English Building. Perhaps a considerate custodian would find his unconscious body and drag him the rest of the way into his office, closing his door and leaving the light off.

Digging deep, H.P. mustered the energy to descend the stairs once again, hoping that there would be no more students with pressing story problems waiting outside his office. When he rounded the corner, what he saw was worse still.

"You look like hell," said Weston. "A guy your age should really get more sleep."

"It's difficult to stay caught up on your sleep when you're detained by the authorities two nights in a row and have to teach classes the next day."

"Then the only reasonable thing to do is quit this job; it's really starting to interfere with our investigation."

"We can't all afford the luxury of being semi-retired." H.P. leaned against his office door as he struggled to fish his keys from his pocket. "So what are you doing here, precisely?"

"Precisely—I'm standing, waiting, talking…but it appears my list is causing you to list, so now I'm helping—vaguely." Weston took the key from H.P.'s tremoring hand and unlocked the door. "Speaking of vaguely helping, while I was waiting for you I had rather an odd chat here in the hallway with one of your students who stopped by. It seems he took your advice and skipped all his classes today to get started writing his novel."

H.P. collapsed into his desk chair. "That wasn't my advice."

"Nevertheless, he was anxious for someone to read the first page he'd written—seemed overly concerned with the title—also happened to mention he'd be spring breaking in Cancun. Don't you usually work on that ramshackle house of yours during the spring and summer breaks? Does it ever bother you that your students live much richer lives than you? Anyway, the young man was eager for my opinion."

"So what did you tell him?"

"To pack plenty of sunscreen and prophylactics. Judging by his personality and pale skin, I figure he'll need a lot of one and none of the other, but when traveling it's always a wise policy to be prepared for any eventuality."

H.P. turned his head toward Weston, only bothering to open one eye to look at him. "You know we are actually trying to educate these people."

"And so I did, potentially saving him from skin cancer and an STD in the process."

"Okay, back to my original—"

"Ed mentioned last night that he was going to ask around on campus today about that shipment of lab equipment. I wanted to see if he turned up any leads."

H.P. sat up in his chair. "Yeah, I was curious about that myself. He should be here now. He's my ride home, and I told him when I'd be done with my last class."

"Maybe he connected with his contacts in the chemistry department this morning after he dropped you off and then went home to take a nap himself, failing to set an alarm."

"Could be…as far as I know, he's still on his stargazing sleep cycle."

"Can you call him at your place?"

H.P. shook his head. "Landlines are so last century…all I need is a cellphone."

"If only someone could convince Ed of that."

Chapter 19

Weston parked behind Kate's car in H.P.'s driveway. "Looks like he forgot to come back to campus and pick you up."

H.P. opened the passenger's side door. "He can be absentminded."

The two climbed the porch steps and entered the house. Weston scanned the cluttered floors and tabletops. "Whoa, this place looks like it's been ransacked."

"No, that's all Ed's stuff," replied H.P. "He's gotten even messier since Kate left—you know how his work is a coping mechanism for him. Curious though, that her car is here but he doesn't appear to be."

"Maybe he's still asleep or in the can."

"He sleeps on the couch, and when he's indisposed, lamentably he's opposed to closed doors, but it looks like the light is off in the bathroom."

"Ed!" Weston shouted. "You here?"

"Perhaps he took one of his telescopes out back."

"It's barely dark."

H.P. stopped cold in the kitchen. "I think Ed's going to need our help—the backdoor's been kicked in."

****

Slim surveyed H.P.'s living room as a couple of county deputies dusted for prints in the kitchen. "So it was like this when you two left this morning?"

"I'm afraid so," answered H.P. "The only thing out of place is that Ed's not here."

Slim nodded. "We've got an APB out on him."

"APB stands for all-points bulletin," said Weston proudly.

H.P. looked daggers at him. "Anyone who can spell APB knows that."

"Listen, you two, this is the third night in a row that you've called me about some situation that's gone gunnysack on you, though I do appreciate you catching me before I fell asleep this time, but you don't have to be no rock scientist to see a pattern brewing. I'm not saying you boys go looking for trouble, but somehow it always seems to find you. Me, local law enforcement, and soon state as well as maybe federal agents will be investigating this matter. Now, I ain't gonna tell you two that you can't do your own snooping around—not because I think saying so isn't the right call, but more because I know it'd be a waste of my breath—but I will say, for Ed's sake, stay out of the way. There are professionals on the case…so go do that thing where you visit bars to follow up on pretend leads or whatever, but—and I'm asking nicely here—keep the hell out of danger and don't muck up the works."

Weston nodded to H.P. "I think we've just been unofficially deputized."

"Oh, I can do better than that," Slim replied. "If you two get into any more trouble, for your own good I'll put you both right back in that jail cell I found you last night, and you can call yourselves honorary wardens."

Chapter 20

Mr. Snide piloted the large SUV down the dark, dirt road while Mr. Whip sat in the passenger's seat doing a crossword puzzle on his phone. "What the hell is an octothorpe?"

"A number sign or pound symbol," answered Mr. Snide. "You know, tiny tick-tack-toe."

"No…it's got to be seven letters."

"Hashtag," said Edwin from the backseat.

Mr. Whip typed the word into the puzzle. "Yep, that's it—thanks."

"No problem, now will you let me go?"

"You seem like a good guy," Mr. Snide said, "but you've gotten yourself mixed up in a bad situation."

Mr. Whip turned around to look at Edwin, who was bound and lying on his side in the backseat. "Trust me, I know from experience that it's cold comfort to hear, but this isn't personal."

"I think it's fair to say that during our short road trip together you've proven yourself to be one of our best-behaved abductees," Mr. Snide added. "After all, we took you at your word that you wouldn't scream if we didn't gag you, and thus far you haven't. We appreciate your cooperation."

"I'm appreciative that you drive an SUV rather than a sedan. I'd hate to be riding on this bumpy road getting bounced around inside a trunk. However, you won't find me so cooperative if your intent is to induce me to divulge Kate's whereabouts. The truth is, I simply don't know."

Mr. Whip turned back around. "I believe him."

Mr. Snide nodded. "Yeah, me too…but he must have a way to contact her somehow."

"No I mustn't," protested Edwin.

"Sorry Edwin," said Mr. Snide. "That I don't believe."

"Well, it's a fact—pain and simple."

"Did you just say 'pain and simple'?" asked Mr. Whip.

"No," answered Edwin.

Mr. Snide smiled. "I heard 'pain' too…must've been a Freudian slut."

"I'm not lying."

"Only duress will tell," replied Mr. Snide.

"Are we going to start in on him tonight?" Mr. Whip asked.

Mr. Snide shook his head. "No, we've been driving all day, and I'm too beat to begin a proper beating. Besides, my experience has taught me that a well-rested subject is a more compliant subject."

"I didn't realize you had experience with this sort of thing."

"What, you never went through boarding school?"

Chapter 21

Weston and H.P. sat at the otherwise unoccupied bar in the Deluxe. Weston swiveled on his stool to assess the tavern. "I think calling this place deluxe qualifies as false advertisement."

The hoary bartender set two mugs of coffee in front of them. "You ain't no prize yourself."

"Don't take it personally," said Weston. "I've definitely been in worse taverns."

"And I've definitely had better-looking customers…nothing personal."

"This is a good place to think." H.P. blew at the steam rising from his mug. "Not at this exact moment, mind you, but usually."

"What are you boys cogitating on tonight?"

"A friend of ours is missing," answered Weston.

"Edwin, the bearded guy you've seen me in here with before, was abducted from my house earlier today."

The bartender wiped the bar with a rag grimier than the bar itself. "Oh yeah, that astronomer fella who almost never buys his own beers. Well, he ain't here."

"We're trying to figure out where his abductors might've taken him." Weston sipped at his coffee.

"Ain't that a matter for the authorities?"

Weston set his mug back on the bar. "You're not the first person to tell us that, but when it comes to this sort of thing, we're not exactly neophytes."

"I can't rightly say I know what that means, but I know well enough when I meet a fella that there's no talking sense to."

H.P. grinned. "He's sure got your number."

"So where do you think they might've taken him?" asked the bartender.

"Could be anywhere," Weston answered.

"Nah, it couldn't be." The bartender held up a smudged glass to the light and wiped at it with his rag until it became pellucid. "We already established that they didn't bring him here—or the moon, I'm guessing—so you can cross those two places off the list. Why'd they take him?"

"To find out where his girlfriend is hiding," answered H.P.

"So not a ransom situation," said the bartender, "which means there's no reason to keep him in town in order to make an exchange and run the risk of someone spotting him. I imagine he'll be reluctant to give up his lady's location, so they probably intend to beat the information out of him. That kind of thing is best done in a secluded place."

"Lots of those around here," Weston said.

"Sure, but kidnapping…we don't get much of that in these parts."

"Thank goodness for small-town favors." H.P. took a sip of coffee.

"Yeah, that sounds like big-city trouble."

H.P. nodded at the bartender. "You're right about that."

"Big-city boys likely wouldn't know the area all that well, but then they also likely wouldn't want to travel too far with someone tied up inside their vehicle—makes getting gas or drive-thru difficult."

Weston stared at the bartender as he considered the line of thinking. "So where do you think big-city kidnappers might set up shop?"

"There's those rental cabins out west of town," replied the bartender. "A lot of hunters drive down from Chicago to stay in them during deer season."

"They could've booked one online," H.P. added.

The bartender nodded. "There's a bunch of 'em, and they're spread out over hundreds of acres of gameland, but it might be a good place to start—especially if you had an inkling as to what kind of vehicle they was driving."

"We do indeed," said Weston, "an Excess-You-Be."

Chapter 22

In the early morning light, Mr. Whip jogged toward Mr. Snide who sat on the small front porch of the cabin. "How far did you go?"

Mr. Whip stretched out his calf muscles on the cinderblock that constituted the single porch step. "Up to the main road…not a soul in sight."

"Your legs okay?"

"A little achy from spending so much of the past few days sitting in that SUV."

"It's the aches that remind us we're not in pain."

Mr. Whip looked up at Mr. Snide. "That almost sounded profound. You can go for a run too if you want—really helps clear out the cobwebs."

"I can't run…my hamstrings are lactic intolerant—allergies, what can you do?"

"Is Edwin awake yet?"

"Yeah," answered Mr. Snide. "I offered him some of our beef jerky for breakfast, but it turns out he's a vegetarian."

"How does a vegetarian get that fat?"

"Too many French fries, I suspect."

"So how do you want to do this?"

"I don't want to do it at all," replied Mr. Snide. "The smart ones are the worst, because they know how it's inevitably going to end, so they hold out the longest."

"Out here we've got plenty of places to bury his body."

"We do at that, but the ground's too cold to dig more than a foot or so. We'll have to burn him. I figure we'll leave his body in the lodge and then set fire to it when we go."

Mr. Whip stretched out his arms over his head. "That makes sense, though I guess the association will have to forfeit the security hold on our corporate credit card."

"I think they can cover it." Mr. Snide stood. "Let's get started with the unpleasant task at hand. He had to use the restroom, so I've got him chained to the back of toilet."

The two entered the diminutive cabin. Mr. Snide knocked on the bathroom door. "Edwin, it's time to come out."

Mr. Whip grabbed Mr. Snide's hand just as he was about to turn the doorknob. "Do you suppose he's in there holding the toilet tank lid, ready to bash whoever opens the door over the head?"

"I don't think he's the type." Mr. Snide pulled his pistol from his waistband. "But better safe than sorry."

Mr. Snide leveled his gun as Mr. Whip pushed open the door. They found the bathroom unoccupied. Where the toilet had been was now a large hole in the floor.

Mr. Snide lowered his gun. "Damnit, the floorboards must've been rotten." He stepped into the bathroom and peered down into the hole at the commode laying on the ground beneath the cabin. "He's still chained and still fat, so he couldn't have gotten far."

"I'll search for him in the woods. You take the SUV and look for him along the road."

Chapter 23

H.P. abruptly sat up in the passenger's seat of Weston's sedan. "Jesus, where are we?"

"Relax—will ya? Are you always this edgy in the morning? No wonder you don't have a woman." Weston yawned. "I got lost driving around on these unmarked backroads in the dark—thanks in no small part to having a sleeping navigator—so I pulled over a couple of hours ago for some shut-eye until daylight."

"Well, it's light now, so let's get moving."

"While I appreciate your enthusiasm, I need to see a man about a horse first." Weston opened his door.

"Urinate with celerity."

"I'd be more inclined to take instruction from you if you hadn't fallen asleep five minutes after we got into the car last night." Weston shut his door and walked around the sedan into a stand of trees on the side of the dirt road. He enjoyed the peaceful, sylvan sounds of early morning as he did his business; however, those sounds were soon interrupted by a large SUV speeding by on the next road over. Weston zipped up and raced back to his car. "I just saw the Excess-You-Be!"

"Where?"

Weston buckled his seat belt. "There's another road not fifty yards from here. In the dark, I didn't even know it was there."

"So let's go."

Weston turned the key in the ignition and sped off, but the road soon came to an end at a crossroad. "Do we go left or right?"

"Which way do you think the SUV went?" asked H.P.

"That was my question."

H.P. shook his head. "I think that's the wrong question. We have a fifty-fifty chance of choosing the correct way the SUV went, or we could go back the direction it came from and give ourselves a much better chance of finding where it had been parked last night."

"That makes sense." Weston turned right and then right again when they came to the next road. They followed the winding road for almost a mile before it dead ended at a small cabin. The two got out to look around.

"There doesn't seem to be anyone here," H.P. observed.

Weston picked up a beef jerky wrapper off the ground. "Somebody was here. This plastic still smells like meat."

"What if the kidnappers are hiding inside, waiting to ambush us?"

"Then I'd say we're well and truly screwed." Weston stopped suddenly and stood silently, listening for a long moment.

"Do you hear something?" whispered H.P.

"Yeah, like a metallic jingle jangle noise."

"I don't hear anything, but with each passing year I have to turn up my TV louder and louder."

"It sounds like it's coming from under the cabin." Weston cautiously approached the front porch, knelt down, and pulled back the cinderblock step.

"Weston," Edwin said softly from the darkness, "is that you?"

"I'm here Ed." Weston reached under the porch. "Stretch out your arms. H.P. come give me a hand."

The two managed to pull Edwin from under the cabin by the chain wrapped around his wrists. They helped him to his feet, and he inhaled deeply. "Now I know how the Wicked Witch of the East must've felt."

"What happened?" asked H.P.

"I'll tell you all about it, but first let's get the hell away from here, though I do want to thank you both for effecting my rescue."

Weston opened the car door for Edwin. "You should thank that senex from the Deluxe too."

"Next time we go there, the tab is on me, and I may even include a gratuity."

Chapter 24

Edwin, wearing a warming blanket over his shoulders, sat on the tailgate of Slim's truck, which was parked in H.P.'s driveway.

Slim worked at the chain wrapped around Edwin's wrists with a bolt cutter. "These links are made of galvanized steel—not the kind of chain used to hold up a porch swing. Them boys weren't messing around." Slim strained to bring the two handles of the bolt cutter closer together until finally the chain broke and fell to the ground.

Edwin stood up from the tailgate and rubbed his sprained wrist. "What a relief it is to be free of my shackles. I don't think I'll ever wear a watch again."

Slim set the bolt cutter in the bed of his pickup. "Okay, county deputies are combing the area around them hunting lodges—"

"But it's a damn big area," said Weston.

"State troopers are on the lookout for a black SUV," Slim continued.

"Which there are about a million of," replied Weston.

"And we didn't catch its license plate number either time we saw it," added H.P.

"And, the feds are trying to trace the credit card used to reserve the lodge."

Weston shook his head. "Which we all know will

turn up exactly nothing."

Slim closed his tailgate. "I hate to admit it, but you're probably right."

"Ed, were you able to find out anything on campus yesterday before you came back here?" H.P. asked.

Edwin nodded. "All the old lab equipment that's being replaced by the shipment of new equipment will be set up at a sort of overflow lab for ongoing experiments...kind of like a commercial kitchen with various groups coming and going and very little oversight."

"Do you think it's worth staking out?" asked Slim.

"Maybe," answered Edwin, "but it'll be weeks yet before it's up and running—not to mention that anyone performing malevolent chemistry there won't be advertising what they're up to, and if you go looking over everyone's shoulder then they'll just start making silly putty instead."

H.P. folded his arms. "Another dead-end."

"Ed, what else can you tell us about the chemical that Kate thought might've been in that missing case?" asked Weston.

Edwin tilted his head back as if he had a nosebleed. "Kate is periodically asked to review data from experiments she's not directly involved with—be a second set of eyes and offer an unbiased opinion about research results. A few months back, she started to notice a pattern of experimentation that, if connected, indicated that testing was underway on something like a panacea—sort of a super vaccine—to address all manner of childhood diseases."

"I don't know much about chemistry, but that sounds like a good thing to me," said Slim.

Edwin nodded. "Such an undertaking would certainly be laudable, but as with all science—the devil is in the details. The work being done, which Kate was privy to, revealed some potentially severe lapses in bioethics, not to mention judgement—using gene drives to modify DNA sequences in order to increase a genome's resistance to any number of pathogens that could cause diseases, ranging from anthrax to Zika."

"I'm loath to echo Slim," Weston said, "but I'm not seeing a problem."

Edwin shook his head. "The problem is off-target mutation. That type of genetic engineering might prove successful at effectively ending hepatitis in future generations, but such DNA recombination also has the potential to unwittingly make tomorrow's children more susceptible to HIV or even lead to the rise of an as yet unknown disease, such as a new strain of smallpox. The complexity and nearly infinite number of ways that sort of tampering can go wrong is why gene manipulation is so dangerous, which is precisely the reason this kind of research ought to be done out in the open under the scrutiny of the scientific community."

"So what's the worst case scenario?" asked H.P.

"About as awful as you can imagine, but the upside is that even though such a so-called super vaccine is theoretically possible, you still have to get it into people's arms. No medical organization in the world would approve such an inoculant without first conducting copious clinical trials to determine the potential side effects."

Weston hooped. "Except that if they managed to introduce such a vaccine into the type of mosquitos that Hooper mentioned, then they could bypass all of that rigamarole, letting the reprogrammed bloodsuckers reproduce and naturally replicate the vaccine as well as administer it."

"And they could also add just about anything else they wanted to their unregulated cocktail," said H.P.

Edwin leaned back against the truck. "That's correct. An entity unprincipled enough to take such drastic measures to foist an untried vaccine on a population likely wouldn't have many qualms about adding other agents to their concoction. After all, their response to the first voice of dissent—so far as we know—was attempting to murder Kate."

"I'd say these skeeters qualify as a pretty bad scenario," Slim said. "So then the case contained…"

"Plasmids, most likely," Edwin answered. "Easily introduced into the bloodstream of an individual— possibly without any deleterious effects to the host— that in turn could be bitten by mosquitos, causing their DNA to mutate, eventually creating swarms of serum spreaders."

"That's so sinister," said Weston.

"I don't necessarily disagree," replied Edwin, "though it's been my experience when dealing with people afflicted by the hubris of science that they tend to be more shortsighted than sinister. Kate had been vacillating for over a week about raising her suspicions to the company's owner, but she was never concerned about her safety—only maybe her job security. I met the owner on several occasions—a kindly old man with silver hair who's involved in a number of children's charities. He certainly shares the scientific community's frustration with the asinine anti-vaxxer movement, but I don't think he would resort to this—or murder, for that matter—to circumvent their inanity. I find it hard to believe that he's behind all this."

"So what should we do?" H.P. asked.

"First thing we do is get you boys someplace safe," answered Slim.

"That seems sensible," Edwin replied. "We've got the two that grabbed me outnumbered now, but they might enlist reinforcements."

"And then what?" asked Weston. "Run? I feel like I've…we've been running from this thing for more than a year now. First they shoot me, then they shoot you, Slim—and they dosed you, H.P., sending you on the craziest drug trip I've ever heard of."

"I did manage to turn that 'trip' into a successful entry in my Pirate Hunter series."

"Not to mention that they destroyed my granddad's house, and your telescope, Ed…and your barn, H.P."

"That thing was really more of an eyesore anyway," replied H.P. "A deathtrap waiting to happen, and so it did."

"I say our days of running are over." Weston clenched his fist and hammered it down onto the tailgate of Slim's pickup. "We should take the fight to them."

"I agree," said H.P. "I think you all should take the fight to them too."

"Them idgits have had us over a barrel for too long, and I wouldn't mind some payback." Slim spit on the ground. "But Weston, don't ever hit my truck again."

Chapter 25

Mr. Snide and Mr. Whip sat in the guest chairs facing an empty desk. Mr. Snide checked his watch. "In two minutes, we'll have been waiting for him for half an hour."

"What do you care?" asked Mr. Whip.

"Back in my day, a man took pride in his work and was at his post when he said he'd be."

"Back in your day? This is your day. You're not that much older than me."

"Then why aren't you more irritated?"

"We get paid the same for sitting as we do for anything else," answered Mr. Whip.

The bald man entered his office as if he'd been catapulted through the door. "Sorry to keep you waiting…traffic was—"

"You know, we're not salesmen," said Mr. Snide. "Our work is important—often literally involving life and death."

The bald man sat down slowly in his desk chair, wearing a bemused expression as he did so. "This is quite a change of tone from our last meeting. What happened to the 'sirs'?"

"Sir, forgive my colleague," said Mr. Whip. "We've been driving up and down the state for much of the past few days, so we're both a little road weary."

The bald man studied the pair for a moment. "I

take it from your expressions that this latest assignment did not go well."

Mr. Whip shook his head. "I'm afraid it did not. We seized the target late yesterday afternoon, but he managed to escape early this morning. We aborted an attempt to reacquire him at his temporary residence when, upon surveilling the farmhouse, we ascertained that an acquaintance of his, a police officer, was at the scene."

"And you weren't able to extract any information from him while he was in your custody?" asked the bald man.

"Negative, sir," Mr. Whip answered.

"Well, gentlemen, this is most disappointing. The association assured me that you are two of their best operatives, but so far, the results of your efforts have left much to be desired."

Mr. Whip raised his index finger to make a point. "Sir, begging your pardon, we did manage to retrieve the case, which was the job we were originally contracted to carry out."

"Yes, you did that part fine…it's the other two parts that you failed to successfully execute—literally." The bald man leaned back in his chair and put his feet up on his desk. "I have one more execution for you…a much easier target, I imagine—my geriatric boss."

"Is that really necessary?" asked Mr. Snide. "According to our intel, he's on his last leg as it is. Why not let him die in peace? Obviously, his being alive hasn't hindered your ability to control his company from behind the scenes."

The bald man put his feet back down on the floor. "I'll remind you that your services were not hired by this company, but rather by the other organization that I represent, which has a longstanding relationship with your association...and, as it happens, there is one additional side task of no small importance that I need you to complete when you go to pay my boss a visit. Accomplish this task, and I'll consider your last couple of missteps a product of poor planning on my part. I'll even submit a satisfactory report to the association on your behalf."

"That's most understanding of you, sir," Mr. Whip replied.

"And what say you, Mr. Snide?"

"Sir, I say that all my years in the military taught me how to use the word 'sir' and not mean it."

Chapter 26

Edwin waited among the snow-covered evergreens near the stables. He blew into his cupped hands to keep his fingers warm.

"You should've worn mittens," Slim said into a walkie-talkie atop a hill some distance off. From a prone position, he scanned the area around the barn with his binoculars. "Your cloudy breath is giving away your location, but I don't see anyone else out and about, so I think you're good."

"Just to be on the safe side," said Weston over a walkie-talkie, "why don't you try not breathing for a while."

Edwin touched his earpiece and then held up his middle finger toward the hilltop on which Slim was posted. "Looks like Ed copied that, Weston."

"I want a walkie-talkie," said H.P. from the passenger's seat of Weston's car, which was parked along the side of the road that ran in front of the sprawling rural property.

Weston turned toward H.P. "They only come in sets of two. Now keep quiet, so that we can hear."

Slim adjusted his binoculars to focus on the side door of the large ranch house. "Heads up, Ed. Looks like you're about to have company. Some fella is walking the path toward the barn...walking pretty slow at that—old timer with a cane."

Edwin gave a thumbs up and then skulked into the stables from the far end. Most of the stalls were empty. As the door closest to the house opened, he crept into the stall nearest the tallest horse and crouched down among the bales of straw.

The old man slowly approached the stall of the tall horse. "How are you today, Aegis?"

The horse whinnied, as if to say, "fine, thanks."

"That's good…you look healthy." He began to brush the horse's coat. "The ranch hands have been doing a nice job of mucking out your stall."

The horse whinnied again.

"I hope this cold snap hasn't made you uncomfortable out here. I can feel the frigidity in my blood, but I think that has more to do with age than the weather."

The horse neighed gently.

"Oh, that's okay…it's part of the journey." The old man began brushing the other side of the horse's neck. "You have most of your life to look forward to. I have most of mine to look back on…at least what I can remember of it. I wish I could watch you race one last time, but Doc—mine, not yours—doesn't think traveling is a good idea, and all the courses around here are closed for the season."

The horse tapped at the floor with his front hoof.

"Don't fret, you'll get your chance to run again. After I'm gone, they'll send you down to the Sunshine State where you can gallop away the warm days with the other thoroughbreds. Until then, you'll stay here with me and your friends where it's quiet…not such a bad life, really."

Edwin stood up. "That's a beautiful stallion, sir."

"Who is that?" asked the old man. "Show yourself."

Edwin stepped around the stall. "I hope I didn't startle you, but—"

"Son, I expect death to visit me any time now…not much startles me these days."

"Do you remember me? My name is Edwin."

"I can't place the name, but your face is familiar."

"I did some work at your facility down the road a ways. It's been a few months since I last saw you. I help Kate from time to time."

"Ah, yes…Kate. How is she?"

"She's in danger, sir." Edwin looked from the old man to the horse. He couldn't interpret either of their expressions. "She has gone into hiding. I'm worried about her."

The elderly gentleman lowered his grooming brush. "That's terrible, son. Is there anything I can do to help?"

Edwin took a step forward. "I was hoping you might have some idea about who's trying to harm her."

"I can't imagine why anyone would want to harm Kate."

"I think it might be someone at your company, sir."

The old man sighed. "I'm sorry to say that it's my company in name only these days. For the past year I've attended various work functions just to get out of the house, but as my condition has advanced, I sensed that my presence was increasingly…unsettling for others."

"Your condition, sir?"

"Alzheimer's…neuroscientists can be surprisingly uncomfortable around people suffering from degenerative brain diseases. Both my parents had it…now it seems it's my turn. That's why I got into neuroscience in the first place…to find a cure, but I guess I ran out of time."

"I'm sorry," said Edwin.

"No need for apologies. I had a good life…did some good things—caused a little trouble. It's ironic…at least, I think so."

"What's that, sir?"

"The key to happiness is learning to cope with life's disappointments. That's why so many successful people are miserable…what drove them to success is what prevents them from being happy."

"That's very interesting, sir." Edwin stepped away from the stall. "I appreciate you taking the time to talk with me."

"Sure thing, son." The old man resumed brushing Aegis. "Stop back by anytime, though I don't promise to remember you being here before."

Edwin exited the barn and waved toward the hilltop.

Slim picked up his walkie-talkie. "Okay, boys, Ed has left the building and is heading back toward the road. I'll be there as soon as I can."

H.P. snatched the walkie-talkie from Weston and depressed the talk button. "Roger that."

Chapter 27

The old man put away the grooming kit and pulled his scarf tight around his neck. As he walked toward the door, Aegis neighed loudly. He turned toward the horse. "Don't worry, I'll be back again tomorrow, God willing."

A man entered through the door at the other end of the barn, letting in an icy gust of air.

"I didn't expect you to return so soon," said the old man. He studied the outline of the figure in the shadows at the far end of the stables, realizing that Edwin had not returned. "Leave here or I shall be forced to call the authorities."

The shadowy figure stood motionless. The old man turned back toward the door and walked as quickly as his cane would allow. The door opened to reveal a tall man blocking his escape. Aegis neighed again.

****

Mr. Whip carried the old man's lifeless body over his shoulder, walking toward the other side of the stables.

"Where are you taking him?" asked Mr. Snide.

"I'm going to toss him in the snow. He has dementia, right? Maybe they'll think he just wandered off and froze to death."

"That's not a bad idea."

Mr. Whip stopped in front of the door and turned

back around. "Who do you think he was referring to when he thought you'd returned 'so soon'?"

"I don't know—could've been somebody from a long time ago," answered Mr. Snide. "Like you say, he has…had dementia."

"Yeah…that makes sense. Okay, you do the other thing while I take him outside to make a snow angel."

"I'm on it."

Mr. Whip opened the door and exited the barn, though a moment later he stepped back inside.

"I guess he didn't wander far." Mr. Snide turned to see that Mr. Whip still had the old man slung over his shoulder.

"There are fresh footprints out there in the snow that lead up to this door."

Mr. Snide grinned. "Yeah genius, they're mine."

"No, I see yours too, but these other prints have a different tread mark in them. You didn't notice them when you came in?"

"Huh, I must've missed them…probably made by one of the ranch hands—or feet, more accurately."

"Sure, probably." Mr. Whip took the old man back out into the cold.

Chapter 28

Weston drove down the interstate, heading for home, as Edwin recapitulated his conversation with the old man from the backseat. "That's why I don't think he's involved…or even knows anything about it."

H.P. turned around in the passenger's seat. "But it's his company."

"Sure," replied Edwin, "though at this point he's more of a figurehead…the nice geriatric guy who shows up for the Christmas party. All the decisions—at least the big ones, I suspect—are made by his vice presidents. Each of whom got their job by taking the initiative, so any one of them might be behind this."

Slim fidgeted, trying to stretch out his long legs in the backseat. "Or all of them."

Edwin nodded. "That's possible…there could potentially be more than one bad actor at play here."

"Does that mean Skeet Ulrich might be involved?" Weston asked.

H.P. ignored Weston's facetious question. "So which VP did Kate report to?"

"None of them exactly," answered Edwin. "She was the de facto head of her own little department, though they all technically had oversight of her operation."

H.P. shook his head. "So we know it's not the owner, but we also know her abduction must've been an inside job—at least to some extent…and that it was most likely a higher up who stood to benefit from her disappearance. I'm afraid that's not much to go on."

"You boys have gone pretty far before on less," said Slim, "and managed to come out smelling like a rose on the other side to boot."

Weston glanced in the review mirror. "Thanks, Slim…though at least half of that was luck."

"Maybe, but it still counts."

Edwin pressed his fingertips together. "What you two told me Hooper had to say about shuffling experiments from one lab to another is interesting. It's long been rumored that there are underground labs conducting surreptitious experimentation, which would help account for the quantum leaps that chemical companies sometimes seem to come up with out of thin air. However, as with Kate's company, lab work is often very fragmented and ad hoc—technicians taking readings and measuring data for larger experiments that have been disaggregated."

H.P. nodded. "Outsourcing the components of off-the-books experiments would be a good way to keep inquisitive minds away from the scent of something illegal, or at least unethical, and create plausible deniability if questions were ever raised."

"Company A does experiment X for company B," said Weston, "and they in turn perform experiment Y for them."

"A regular do-si-do of bad science," added Slim.

"Yes, but the enormity of the task to coordinate such a square dance is staggering," replied Edwin. "The whole point of a scenario like that is for no one chemical company to know too many of the secrets."

"But what if none of them did?" asked H.P. "What if the coordination is handled by another group?"

"Kind of a clearinghouse of evil chemistry," Weston added.

Slim whistled softly. "That would go a long way to explain the connection between your run-in with king corn and, H.P., your dealings with them nightmare drugs."

"So maybe if we find the loose cannon in Kate's company and pull at that loose thread," H.P. said, "we'll unravel the whole mystery."

As they lost reception to the station they'd been listening to, Weston turned the tuner knob on the radio. "You're mixing metaphors like a Cuisinart, but you might be on to something."

"Can we listen to the rest of that one?" asked H.P.

"Alice Cooper?" Weston turned up the volume. "You don't seem the type."

"It's a good song," said H.P.

"I didn't say it wasn't a good song; I'm saying you don't seem the type."

The four sat in silence as they listened to the end of the song. "You're listening to WBBN. I'm your deejay J.D., which stands for Just Don't…as in, change that dial—cuz I'm here to put the *ass* in classic rock. This just in from the news desk, local chemical magnate and philanthropist found dead outside his home in the greater Chicagoland area."

Weston turned down the volume. "No more Mr. Nice Guy."

Chapter 29

Mr. Snide walked from the rest stop to their SUV with two cups of vending-machine coffee. Mr. Whip closed his laptop as Mr. Snide opened the driver's side door and placed the Styrofoam cups in the center console. "I got you one."

Mr. Whip picked up a cup, removed the lid, and circumspectly eyed the coffee. "You know, the reason you have to stop every hour is because you keep drinking this stuff."

"No, the reason I have to stop every hour is because I'm over 50." Mr. Snide buckled his seat belt. "When I was your age, I could drink a gallon of coffee without having to hit the head for hours, but if I don't drink coffee these days, I can't keep my eyes open after an hour or so of driving—sort of a catch-22 of aging."

"I've never understood that expression."

"It's from a book that was popular with my generation."

"*Catcher in the Rye*?"

Mr. Snide sipped his coffee, letting it burn the acerbic remarks from his tongue. "So, any updates from the association?"

Mr. Whip tucked his laptop under the passenger's seat. "Yeah, apparently the Egghead wants to meet again."

"Twice in one day? People are going to start asking

questions if we keep going into his office."

"You and the Egghead must be of like minds. On the association work order, he requested that we stop by his home after dinnertime."

"After dinnertime?" Mr. Snide glanced at his watch. "Jesus, I like it so much better when we don't interact directly with the client. I'm surprised he didn't request that we come over before dinner and pick him up some takeout along the way…maybe fetch his damn dry cleaning for him while we're at it. I mean, how else can we accommodate this clown? The association explained that we're not his errand boys, right?"

"Ours is not to question why."

"Actually the line is, 'Ours is not to reason why.' It's from a Tennyson poem, and the Charge of the Light Brigade didn't exactly end well for the cavalry soldiers."

"I think you might've missed your calling." Mr. Whip blew the steam rising from his coffee. "You should've been a college professor or something."

"Nah, it wouldn't have worked out. As a young man I was footloose and full of wanderlust. A flak jacket was a better fit for me than a tweed one."

"We've got a couple of hours. Why don't you hop in the back to get some kip, and I'll drive us out to the Egghead's place?"

"I don't nap on the job." Mr. Snide started up the SUV. "Besides, you're the brawn and I'm the brains, so I drive in case we get pulled over and I have to dissemble, and you ride shotgun in case you have to jump out to dismember."

"You just don't want me deciding where we stop for dinner, do you?"

"I don't like the coffee at the places you pick."

Chapter 30

Weston opened the front door as Becky came down the stairs with Ance. She toddled across the living room to hug her daddy's leg. He picked her up and kissed his wife. "I've missed you two."

Becky hugged him. "Us too. It's been like the bad old days with police cars driving by the house every ten minutes."

Slim entered with several bags and closed the door behind him. "Sorry about that, Miss Becky. I put a call in to the station, but there's probably nothing to be concerned about."

"That's what you told us last time." Becky watched as the front door opened again.

"Hello, Becky," said Edwin.

"Ed, I'm so glad you're all right…and I see you've brought a sleeping bag."

Edwin raised the sleeping bag, as if he'd forgotten he was carrying it. "Slim suggested we all stay in one place so that he can better keep an eye on us."

H.P. entered with a sleeping bag as well. "Yes, and apparently the bad guys already know where I live."

"And we couldn't stay at Slim's," said Weston, "since he lives in a barn."

"Some say I was born in a barn, on account of my manners," replied Slim, "but my bachelor pad is currently parked next to a barn and would not accommodate four grown men."

"So you're all staying here?" Becky turned to Weston. "You might've called."

"I was worried that if I called, you'd have all the locks changed before we got here." Weston waited for a smile. Not getting one, he continued on. "We brought dinner—a trunk full of Thai food."

"Yeah, the Thai place in town is going out of business," added Slim. "He ordered one of everything and they threw in their 'We're Open' sign."

Weston put his arm around his wife. "It lights up even."

"Too bad they didn't give you a 'No Vacancy' sign instead. I could've hung it in the window."

Edwin broke the silence that followed first. "So can we eat now?"

Becky glared at him. "Oh, shut the front door!"

****

"Mr. Edwin," said Lance from across the dining room table, "you study things in the sky, right? Do you know much about balloons?"

Van shook his head. "Not this again."

"In college I used data collected by radiosondes that were tethered to weather balloons for my research on how atmospheric conditions affected the functioning of optical telescopes."

Lance set down his milk. "Great, you sound like the person to ask then. We were watching the Rose Bowl Parade on TV a few weeks ago, and there were no balloons like there were for the Thanksgiving Day parade…but they had all these floats—and none of them floated. It was very disappointing."

"You're ridiculous," said Van.

"Well, you're ridicu-more," replied Lance.

"That's your influence on them." Becky turned from Weston to her youngest son. "Buddy, we've talked about this before…it's just what they're called— let it go."

Lance poked at the noodles on his plate. "If I let go of a balloon it'll float away, but if I let go of a float it won't go anywhere."

"Young scholar, you've identified an interesting bit of irony," H.P. said, "but I don't think Ed will be much help since he doesn't know irony from ferrum."

Edwin grinned. "Ferrum is the Latin name for iron, atomic number 26; it's the most common element on Earth by mass."

"So then I guess you guys can't help me with my question about why they call them sweaters and slippers either?" asked Lance.

Weston dropped his chopsticks on his plate. His hands trembled, and his eyes rolled back in his head. He emitted a low yowl, like a banshee in need of a career change.

"Should we consult a doctor?" H.P. asked, "or perhaps a medium?"

"He's not possessed," replied Van. "He's just time traveling."

"He does this about once a week or so," Lance added, "but he always acts as if it's the first time."

"The mind of the man seated before you has been transported into the future," Weston said in an eerie voice.

Edwin smiled. "So that's where you've been keeping it."

"I see a large man…sort of a Santa Claus type sans

the jolliness. He stares at the vast sky through a tiny hole as others more conveniently study stars much farther away on computer screens."

"I think your telescopes are neat, Mr. Edwin," said Lance.

"Thank you, Mr. Lance."

"I see that the one named Lance Delacroix has become a world-famous etymologist, creating a new language free of absurdity. Now the world communicates with ease…and finally realizes that no one has all that much to say."

Ance giggled at her father's antics.

"I see the littlest one now, Ance Payley—fully grown, beautiful and charming like her mother. She's feeding mush on a spoon to her daddy the way he once fed her. Does he make a mess of his shirt because he can no longer control his mouth, or is it merely payback?"

"Based on this display, I'm wagering on the former," said H.P.

"I see an old, very sad man. He writes stories in the attic of a dilapidated farmhouse, longing for the days of artistic invigoration he enjoyed many years before during his collaboration with a writer who he both revered and envied."

Slim picked up his beer. "This is some parlor trick."

"I see the one formerly known as Slim, who now goes by Pudgy. He spends his days fishing and drinking beer…so not much has changed for him aside from his waistline."

Slim set his beer back down. "On second thought, maybe this isn't so great."

"Oh, go ahead and do me." Becky took a sip from her wine glass.

Weston opened one eye to look at her. "I think for our guests' sake we should finish dinner first."

"What about Van?" asked Lance.

"The fog is growing thicker...it's getting harder to see. Did Vance Delacroix raise his grades enough to get into college? Did he apply himself when it came to completing those college applications? It's foggier now...but wait, I see him—standing proudly with a diploma in one hand and a paycheck in the other, which he intends to use to take his mother and her exceptionally handsome husband out to dinner."

Becky set down her wine glass. "Ugh, I didn't know getting remarried again was in my future."

Chapter 31

The Egghead walked upstairs to change into his pajamas when he noticed a light coming from under the door to his study.

"Hon, the overture has started," his wife called up from the living room.

The Egghead opened the study door and was startled to see Mr. Whip perusing his collection of framed theater memorabilia and Mr. Snide sitting behind his desk. "How did you—"

"Hon?"

The Egghead stepped back into the hallway and leaned over the banister. "I'll be down in a few minutes. I forgot I need to send a couple of work emails." He reentered his study. "How the hell did you guys get in here?"

"This is a large house, sir." Mr. Whip took a seat on a wingback chair near the balcony. "You might be having dinner with your wife downstairs and not even realize that people were waiting for you upstairs."

"You really ought to extend your house alarm system to the second floor," added Mr. Snide, "especially given some of the choices you've made in your professional life."

"I'll take it under advisement." The Egghead sat in the room's other wingback chair. "I'd offer you two something from my liquor cabinet, but it looks like

121

you've already made yourselves at home."

Mr. Snide shook his head. "We don't drink on the job."

"So what did you want to see us about, sir?"

"I wanted to find out how things went with my boss—"

"You didn't hear about his untimely passing on the news?" asked Mr. Snide.

"I did…however, in addition, I had a thought about how to reacquire Edwin."

Mr. Snide leaned back in the desk chair. "In the future, feel free to share any thoughts you may have with your association contact, who'll be sure to relay them to us if they're of value."

"Trust us—it's more efficient that way, sir."

"Duly noted," replied the Egghead. "It's just that I asked the association to provide me with some background on Edwin after his…escape, and it seems he's friends with a couple of novelists from downstate."

Mr. Whip nodded. "We read that same dossier, sir."

"In fact, we acquired Mr. Hubert at one of their homes," added Mr. Snide.

"But what you probably haven't read is my latest alumni magazine." The Egghead pointed to the open magazine atop his desk, which featured a photo of Weston and H.P. "His two friends collaborated on a book and are giving a reading tomorrow in Indianapolis. I figure there's a good chance Edwin might tag along."

Mr. Whip turned to Mr. Snide. "Could be lots of people there…people sometimes get lost in crowds."

Mr. Snide took the magazine from the desk and

rolled it up. "We'll look into it, but next time give the tip to your association contact."

"Next time, ring the damn doorbell." The Egghead stood. "I assume you two can show yourselves out the way you came in."

Chapter 32

Weston and Slim waited over a brewing pot of coffee in the kitchen. Weston took a couple of mugs from a cupboard and set them on the counter. "What are you up to today?"

"I'm going to check in at the station, maybe follow up on a couple of leads, and then spend a good chunk of my day parked out front in the driveway."

"Sounds exciting," said Weston.

"Excitement ain't something you need to worry about…at least not until we get this thing sorted out. I want you three here—away from any excitement and out of trouble."

H.P. wandered into the kitchen. "Don't forget we've got that book reading at noon."

"Reading?" asked Slim.

Weston nodded. "Yeah, it's this activity that involves a lot of left to right, but it's not done much around here, so I don't blame you for not being familiar with it."

"You boys ain't going to no damn book reading today."

"But if we don't show, we'll surely disappoint a dozen or so mildly ardent fans," said Weston.

"It's been scheduled for over a month." H.P. took a coffee mug from the counter. "It'd be very poor form to cancel the day of."

Slim took the other mug. "I could care less about poor form."

"Meaning you care some," Weston said, "meaning we can go?"

"It's in Indiana," added H.P. "No one will be looking for us there."

"Besides, what bad thing ever happened in Indiana aside from Larry Bird leaving the state to play ball in Boston?" asked Weston. "We'll kiss a few prized pigs, stare at some empty cornfields along the way, and be back in time for dinner."

"What about Edwin?" asked Slim.

"He can come along," answered H.P. "We'll keep an eye on him."

"I don't think you quite get how these things work." The light on the coffee machine switched off, and Weston filled Slim's and H.P.'s mugs. "The audience will be comprised almost exclusively of cat ladies who're bored with knitting at home and frail wannabe writers who live in fear of direct sunlight."

Slim blew at the steam rising from his coffee and then set it back on the counter. "I don't like it, and I still intend to keep watch over you three, so call me if you get into any trouble."

Edwin ambled into the kitchen and took Slim's mug off the counter. "I thought I smelled coffee brewing."

"Ed, what do you think about taking a road trip today?" asked H.P.

"That'll be quite a change of pace. See, I know how irony works."

H.P. shook his head. "That's more sarcasm, but I suppose we're splitting hairs."

"Why in the world would we want to bifurcate jackrabbits?"

Weston smiled. "Let's work a little more on irony before we transition to idioms."

"You seem to be in a good mood," Edwin replied. "Did you get lucky sleeping under your own roof last night?"

Weston pulled two more mugs from the cupboard. "Having sex isn't called 'getting lucky' when you're married with children...it's called getting extremely lucky. By the way, Becca hates that joke."

Chapter 33

Mr. Snide drove into Indianapolis as Mr. Whip wiped the sleep from his eyes. "I wish the association would let us stay in nicer accommodations. I was awake half the night listening to people using the ice machine down the hall."

"That kept me awake too, but still it beats sleeping in barracks," said Mr. Snide. "Though I was tempted to stick my head out the door and yell, 'Stop icing down whatever booze you're drinking and just drink it straight from the bottle. You'll pass out sooner, and we'll all get more sleep.'"

"Really? I was tempted to just shoot them."

"When all you have is a gun, every problem seems like a target."

Mr. Whip grinned. "You're full of profound thoughts in the morning."

"My ex-wife used to say that too…then she'd tell me I should sleep in more."

"Ex-wife? I didn't realize you'd gotten a divorce, but then it's been a while since we've worked together."

"Too much time away from home resulted in the all too predictable."

Mr. Whip studied the traffic. "I'm sorry to hear that."

"I made the mistake of leaving out my association

computer, and she made the mistake of trying to check her email. They alerted me to an unauthorized user; I didn't recognize the email address she used, so I did some digging and discovered she had an online dating account. Here I thought maybe she was sleeping with our neighbor, but it turns out she was screwing half the town."

"That's a punch in the gut."

"Every time I open that damn laptop, I recall every word of betrayal in her emails, but that's what I get for marrying a much-younger woman. She tried to explain it all as some sort of protest against my protracted absences…as if her sleeping around somehow proved how much she missed me. I told her, 'You thought so little of our marriage that you repeatedly dishonored it, but now that all those indiscretions have come to light, I'm expected to value our union so highly that I look the other way?'"

"Ouch."

Mr. Snide shook his head. "No, the ouch came when she threatened to tell the reptilian divorce attorney she hired about the actual source of my income. I explained to her that she was entitled to some of my money, but if she revealed how I really earned a living, then neither of us were ever going to be able to spend any of it."

"Did she see it your way?"

"Sure…after I cut the brake line on her car."

"What's that you told me a moment ago about 'every problem'?" asked Mr. Whip.

"I wasn't trying to snuff her exactly…I disabled her brakes, not the airbags—just wanted to send her a message is all. She'll be fine…eventually." Mr. Snide steered the SUV into the crowded bookstore parking lot. "There're a lot more people here than I anticipated."

Chapter 34

"There're a lot more people here than I anticipated." Weston drove H.P. and Edwin into the bookstore parking lot. "Do you want me to drop you two at the door?"

H.P. shook his head. "No, we should stick together. Besides, last time I was here they had me park in the back."

Weston drove around to the rear of the store. "I didn't realize you'd given readings in Indiana before."

"Sure, lots of times."

"No wonder your book sales are so low."

"Listen, you've got to cool it with the illiterate Indiana cracks. Hoosiers take a lot of pride in their state, and your incendiary remarks are liable to set them off."

"Kurt Vonnegut was born here," Edwin added from the backseat.

H.P. nodded. "I wouldn't be surprised if all these people are here because they caught wind of what you had to say during our radio interview."

"Too bad we weren't interviewed for the campus paper instead. If my comments had been in print, these Indianapolans probably would've never known about them."

H.P. tugged at his earlobe. "They're going to come after us with torches and pitchforks."

"I imagine those qualify as advanced weaponry around here."

Edwin chuckled. "That's a good one."

H.P. turned to look at Edwin. "To paraphrase an old punch line: I don't have to outrun the angry mob, I just have to outrun you."

****

The bookstore manager escorted the three through the stockroom. "We're so pleased you've arrived safely. We've never had a turnout like this before."

Weston looked over at H.P. "You hear that? Our reputations precede us."

"I think it might also have something to do with a few remarks you made earlier this week that may have rubbed people around here the wrong way." The manager stopped at the door to the sales floor. "Your lectern is just through there."

"Aren't you going to introduce us?" asked H.P.

The manager placed a hand on the back of his neck. "Uh...well, as your friend mentioned, your reputations precede you, so I don't think introductions are necessary."

"We're still a few minutes early," said Weston. "Should we wait a bit to give everyone time to settle down?"

The manager shook his head. "I don't think that's going to happen...and frankly, it'd probably be better if we just got this over with."

"I don't have to go out there, do I?" asked Edwin.

Chapter 35

Mr. Snide and Mr. Whip stood next to a display of discount calendars. Mr. Whip scanned the crowd. "Do you see them?"

"What are you asking me for, treetop?" asked Mr. Snide. "All I see are the backs of heads."

The restive crowd erupted in boos and hisses as the door to the stockroom swung open.

The next sound was that of Weston's amplified voice. "Quiet, please. This is a bookstore, not a tractor pull. I understand that some of you might be upset by remarks that were allegedly made by one of us. I can't speak for H.P., but in my defense, I'd like to offer some context around the statements you may have heard me make...you see, I'm an asshole."

"You're damn right about that," someone shouted from the meditation section.

"See, there are some things we can agree on," Weston replied. "Now that we're all on the same page, my accomplice...sorry, co-conspirator...apologies again, co-author and I would like to read a short—"

The hand of a militant young woman in the front row shot up. "I have a question."

Weston shook his head. "Miss, I believe this store has a no-smoking policy, so on behalf of the management I'll thank you to keep that steam from coming out of your ears. Typically at a book reading,

132

questions are saved until the end, but I understand if this is all new for most of you, so in the spirit of détente please go ahead."

"I write for the local college newspaper, and I—"

Weston nodded. "Color me impressed. I didn't realize this city had either of those things."

"Are you mocking my hometown, sir?" asked the young woman.

"I haven't been knighted yet, so there's no need to call me sir. But sincerely, I think it's terrific that this community has chosen to embrace literacy and higher education.

"Sure, there will always be those naysayers who'll try to make you feel less than, but don't let elites like those from the so-called prestigious university where my friend teaches just up I-74 convince you that your institutions aren't of the same caliber. The goal of places like that is to impose an intellectual caste system on all of us just to make themselves feel superior, looking down their noses from their ivory towers to tell the rest of us that somehow we're not on the same level as them.

"They're obsessed with arbitrary rankings, what with their admission policies that strip applicants of their individuality and replace them with stats such as GPAs and ACTs. Numbers shouldn't define us. Do you know who else liked to label human beings with numbers? Nazis. So let them make a big deal out of some silly SAT score, but what I want to know is if they've heard of three other letters that are important to me and I suspect might be of importance to you too: USA."

H.P. rolled his eyes at the déjà vu all over again. "I

promise we've heard of it."

"They've 'heard of it' he says." Weston turned from H.P. to the crowd. "But did they listen? Listen to how we're all created equal…that we're all entitled to the pursuit of happiness—just so long as you don't try to pursue it at their snobby university, I suppose."

Several in the crowd clapped and someone whistled, but the co-ed reporter was having none of it. "That's not an answer to my question—you're deflecting."

Weston grinned. "I don't know if you're the good kind of trouble or the bad kind of trouble, but I can tell you're definitely trouble."

"Now you're redirecting," said the reporter.

"Would you say it's working?"

The reporter smiled. "Maybe a little."

"You're a spitfire, aren't you? When I was a younger man, I liked 'em kinda crazy. Not, you know, 'what've you done with my penis?' crazy…but a bit of spice is nice—keeps things interesting."

Many in the crowd chuckled at Weston's ribald comment. An old woman shouted, "Pull a nickel from behind her ear." More people laughed.

Weston beckoned the young woman to join him behind the lectern. "H.P. and I write a lot of dialogue, so we'd intended to read a scene for you today involving the Pirate Hunter and the Spinster, but to continue in the spirit of burying the hatchet, why don't you come up here and read the Spinster part and I'll read the Pirate Hunter?"

The crowd cheered. People seated around the reporter prodded her to go stand next to Weston. When she did so the cheering grew louder.

As H.P. stepped behind Weston to make room for the reporter, he said in a hushed tone, "Yeah, you really buried the hatchet—right into my back."

Weston patted H.P. on the shoulder. "Hey, every book I sell is a book you sell—besides, this beats getting beaten up."

Chapter 36

As Weston merged onto the interstate, Edwin looked out the rear window, instinctively searching for car grilles featuring star emblems, such as Subarus and Mercedes. "I must say, that went better than I expected."

H.P. twisted around in the passenger's seat. "What were you expecting?"

"A scene from *The Day of the Locust*," Edwin answered without turning from his task.

"I never saw that one," said Weston.

H.P. faced forward again. "Me neither, but I remember the movie poster."

"I think the two guys that kidnapped me are following us," Edwin said in an even tone.

Weston glanced in his rearview mirror. "Are you being serious?"

"I'm serious, but I'm not certain…it looks like the same SUV, though it was dark both times I saw it. The two people sitting in the front seem to be of the same proportions as my abductors, though it's hard to see much detail at this distance with the sun reflecting off their windshield."

H.P. turned around to have a look. "You seem rather nonchalant about the possibility of it being them."

"There's no reason to be otherwise until the

possibility becomes an actuality. Besides, they can't kidnap me again—not while I'm inside a car traveling at highway speeds."

"They could shoot at us," said H.P.

"Oh, I hadn't considered that."

Weston checked his sidemirrors and then his rearview mirror again. "Ed, I see the SUV you're talking about, but it doesn't appear to be in a hurry to catch up to us."

Edwin faced the front. "Try accelerating to see if they speed up."

****

"You're tailing them too close," said Mr. Whip.

Mr. Snide shook his head. "If I fall back any farther, we might lose them in all this traffic. We really ought to have two vehicles for this type of thing."

"Is that Edwin in the backseat?"

Mr. Snide squinted. "I can't tell with the glare from the rear window, but if somebody's in the backseat, it stands to reason that there are three people in the car, and my money is on Edwin being the third wheel."

"Maybe, but the way Weston threw H.P. under the bus at that reading, I wouldn't be surprised if he chose not to sit up front on the drive home...or even decided to hitchhike for that matter."

"Yeah...that was way more raucous than any reading I've ever attended. If I were in Edwin's shoes, I probably would've stayed out of sight too."

Mr. Whip pointed. "They're speeding up. I told you we were following them too closely."

"Right now, I really wish you were in a second vehicle." Mr. Snide stepped on the accelerator. "Any more 'I told you so' comments and I'll let you out on the side of the road. Perhaps you and H.P. can hitchhike together."

****

"They've sped up," said Edwin.

Weston studied the SUV in his rearview mirror. "I see them."

Edwin put on his seat belt. "Their vehicle must weigh considerably more than your sedan. We can outrun them, right?"

"In theory," Weston answered, "but with all this traffic around, it's not exactly optimal drag race conditions, though this is Indianapolis, and we are on a beltway, so maybe making a right turn would be enough to shake them."

"Could you take this a little more seriously?" asked H.P.

"I am…I'm going to call in the calvary." Weston dialed a number on his mobile phone and set it in the cupholder.

"Jell-O," said Slim's voice through the phone's speaker.

"Slim, you told us to call if we got into trouble. You might've been right that coming here was a mistake."

"What's your 20, and what's the situation?"

"We're in a westbound lane on the northern leg of I-465," answered Weston, "and we're pretty sure the bad guys are in pursuit."

"Okay, first thing—get off the interstate."

"Are you sure about that, Slim?" H.P. asked. "There's a lot of cars around, so maybe they won't try anything with all these witnesses."

"Trust me, if they start shooting, most of those

witnesses are going to panic and slam on their brakes, causing a traffic jam that'll cut off all your exit routes, which will make you sitting ducks. Your best bet is to keep them in your rearview mirror and get to a less-congested area. In fact, I have just such an area in mind."

****

Mr. Whip held his pistol on the armrest as Mr. Snide passed cars in both the left and right lanes. "This thing handles like a bus."

"We don't have to overtake them," said Mr. Whip. "Just get me close enough to shoot out a tire, and then we'll nab Edwin from the wreckage."

"That'll be messy."

"We're not being paid for our neatness."

Mr. Snide leaned over the steering wheel for a better look. "Wait, are they signaling?"

"Yeah…it looks like they're slowing down."

"I don't imagine they intend to pull off onto the shoulder and just turn Edwin over?"

Mr. Whip shook his head. "No, it looks like they're pulling into that rest area up ahead, even though the sign says it's under construction and not due to open until the spring."

"When you've got to go, you've got to go." Mr. Snide slowed to pull off as well.

"They're driving through the parking lot and taking that gravel road past all the construction equipment."

"It probably just leads to that empty field up on the hill. Why give up the advantage of paved roads? It's like they're trying to make this easy for us."

"Maybe we spooked 'em," said Mr. Whip. "People do dumb things when they're scared."

"My experience has been that people do dumb things all the time, but you might be right."

"We're gaining on them now."

Mr. Snide nodded. "I think we should be able to catch them just over that ridge."

"Do you hear something?"

"Not with all this road noise, but then you've got younger ears. What are you hearing?"

"Like a...lawnmower."

"This time of year?" Mr. Snide gripped the steering wheel tighter. "They're on the other side now, so keep an eye out for them as we go over the top."

As the SUV crested the ridge, its windshield became obscured by a large, fast-moving object. Mr. Whip reflexively ducked. "Holy Jesus, what was that?"

Mr. Snide stopped the SUV for a better look, staring up into the sky. "If I had to hazard a guess, I'd say a Cessna 150, and it appears to be circling around for another pass."

Mr. Whip looked up as well. "Huh, it's not a very big plane."

"It was big enough a moment ago when you tried to dive under the dashboard."

"It startled me is all, but it's just a prop plane. I say we keep after them."

Mr. Snide turned the SUV around. "What, you never saw *North by Northwest*?"

"No, but I remember the poster."

As they crested the ridge in the opposite direction, Mr. Snide stopped the SUV again. "I think we've been had."

Mr. Whip pointed at the state troopers pulling into the rest area below with their light bars flashing.

"Where the hell did they come from?"

"Probably radioed in by Sky King up there...speaking of which, here he comes again. I suppose that means it's time to go off-road." Mr. Snide pulled onto the frozen field, quickly accelerating away from the rest area.

Chapter 37

Slim taxied over to where Weston had parked along the gravel road, his plane's tundra tires leaving tracks in the snowy patina that covered the field. Once the plane's propeller sputtered to a stop, Slim exited the aircraft. "I chased them boys for a long ways, but they hightailed it into some woods, and I lost 'em."

"Then what good are you?" Weston hopped off the hood of his sedan. "Seriously though, thanks for the save."

"Yes," agreed Edwin, "it was most fortunate for us that you decided to fly into Indy and standby at the airport."

"Air cav to our rescue," added H.P.

Slim kicked at a clump of frozen dirt with his boot. "I had nothing better to do today."

"The state troopers told us they'd be on the lookout for the license plate number you radioed to them," said Edwin.

"That's good and all," replied Slim, "but I don't figure much will come of it. I bet them boys are slipperier than snakes slathered in lard."

"Then how do we catch them before they slither back?" asked H.P.

Slim smiled. "I like your spirit. The trick is to stop the one who first let them off the leash."

Weston shook his head. "I loathe to interrupt the

makings of a tragically mixed metaphor that will hopelessly confuse Ed, but we've gotten about as far at identifying the puppet master in all this as we have of IDing those unleashed limbless lizards."

"We know it's probably someone high up enough in Kate's company to make decisions with impunity," H.P. said, "at least so far."

"I got an email last night that there will be a memorial at the company's compound later today to mourn the passing of the owner," said Edwin. "Most of the employees will be there—certainly all the executives."

Weston turned to Slim. "I think this is typically the point when you say something like, 'You boys are fittin' to get into more trouble than a racoon in a crocodile swamp.'"

"Coons are native to North America," Slim replied. "Crocodiles are not...you're probably thinking of alligators. Anyways, I don't reckon it's such a bad idea. Obviously, Ed shouldn't go, seeing how he's known to whoever's behind all this, but you two might be able to fly under the radar since you ain't met nobody at the company personally, at least so far as we know. Besides, I could connect with law enforcement up in them parts to ensure that we have eyes on you at all times while you're there—just to make sure everybody stays friendly like."

Weston looked over at H.P. "What do you think? Feel like crashing a memorial service?"

"So long as it doesn't turn into ours."

Slim rubbed his knuckles. "This might just be the best shot we have to flush this pheasant from hiding before he sics his lapdogs on Ed again."

"Wait," said Edwin, "is the pheasant holding the leash of both the dogs and the snakes while simultaneously pulling the strings of a puppet?"

Weston smirked. "See, what'd I tell you?"

Chapter 38

Mr. Snide steered the SUV on three flat tires and a bare rim into a rural gas station. He parked near the side of the garage. "I'll see about procuring us a new vehicle. You keep trying to get through to the association."

Mr. Whip looked up from his laptop. "What do I tell them if I get a signal?"

"Tell them we're snafued, which is an apt description for this whole assignment as far as I'm concerned."

Mr. Snide rounded the corner of the garage. The sound of an impact drill echoed through the open bay door. A grease monkey under a truck up on a lift turned to look at him. "Can I help you, mister?"

"I'm having some issues with my SUV."

"Yeah, I noticed the sparks when you pulled in."

"The interior's still in good shape. Anything I might be able to trade it in for? I'm not particular, just so long as it runs."

"This ain't a used car lot."

"I hear you, but you see we're in sort of a hurry to get back on the road."

"Is that your automobile to be trading?"

"In point of fact, no," answered Mr. Snide. "But I can promise you that the rental agency won't come looking for it. It's probably better, given the circumstances, if I don't turn it back in, so my…company will just cover the cost of the vehicle with them outright."

"Okay, I ain't gonna ask you no more questions about that then."

"Much obliged."

The grease monkey wiped his hands on his overalls. "I'm nearly done fixing the tranny on this here truck, but it's been in my family for thirty odd years now."

"Ah, so it holds some sentimental value for you?"

"I guess you might say that."

"Then I suggest an exchange of my SUV for your pickup, and I'll throw in a thousand dollars for sentimentality's sake."

The grease monkey eyed Mr. Snide's suit. "This truck ain't even worth half that, but then you told me you was in a bind, so I say your vehicle and an extra two grand."

With a menacing aspect, Mr. Snide stuck his hand into his coat pocket. "How brave we are in the big moments; how scared we are in the small ones. If only we were better at discerning the difference."

"You know what, let's just call it an even trade— my truck for your SUV. I don't need the extra money…or any trouble."

"Have it your way." Mr. Snide removed his hand from his pocket to reveal a roll of candy. "Want a LifeSaver?"

Chapter 39

Weston parked in the lot of the compound's main building.

Slim radioed into his and H.P.'s earpieces. "I'm just on the other side of the perimeter fence, and I've got a clear visual on you two."

Weston saluted toward the fence as H.P. touched his earpiece. "I didn't think this thing would be so uncomfortable."

Weston turned toward H.P. "What?"

"This earpiece...it's bigger than I thought."

"Yeah, makes it so I can only hear out of one ear."

"Do you think people will notice it?" asked H.P.

"Maybe...though they'll likely assume it's a hearing aid."

"I suppose my hearing being diminished by half will only serve to support that assumption."

Weston nodded. "Sure...that and your age."

"I'll remind you that we're the same age."

"Some of us wear our years better than others."

"Are you boys gonna gab all damn day or actually go inside?" Slim asked.

The two exited Weston's sedan, and H.P. gave a thumbs-up.

"Put that thing away," Weston admonished. "You look like a hitchhiker."

"All right, boys," Slim said, "we've got the officer

at the front gate, one in the control room monitoring the cameras inside the building, and several others stationed around the perimeter. If something starts to go sideways, you won't have to look to find us."

The large, crowded lobby of the building put one in mind of a fancy hotel rather than a science facility. H.P. whistled softly. "I definitely went into the wrong profession."

"You mean teaching storytelling to liberal arts students isn't as lucrative as creating potentially mind-altering chemicals that may also cure diseases? Say it ain't so."

"Remind me later to kick you in the shin."

"Okay," said Slim, "I just got word from the control booth that you're on TV—but don't go waving at the cameras."

H.P. scanned the group gathered around the waterfall fountain as Weston eyed the buffet table. "I suppose we should split up and mingle."

"In your case, I think you mean nosh," H.P. replied, "but it's not a bad idea—just remember this is a solemn occasion, so be on your best behavior…or a bit better than that if you can manage it."

"You're such a den mother." Weston headed toward the buffet. Rather than attacking the trays of food from the side of the table, he dutifully waited in line at the end of the table and took a little plate when it was his turn. He used tongs to take several shrimp; he added a small dollop of caviar to his plate, as well as some crackers, grapes, and a few cubes of cheese. Then he turned and spilled his plate down the front of a woman's black dress. "My apologies." He instinctively wiped at her torso the way he might clean his daughter, but then thought better of it and handed over his napkin. "Perhaps I ought to let you do that."

The woman accepted his napkin. "Thank you, and it's me who should apologize. I was attempting a boardinghouse reach of a shrimp cocktail, but I should've waited in line like you and not been in such a hurry."

"I'd offer you mine, but—" Weston knelt to pick up his shrimp off the floor.

"Oh, you needn't bother with that." The woman pointed toward a uniformed man approaching with a dustpan. "The catering crew will take care of it."

"But it's my mess."

"I think more accurately it's our mess, but it's his job." The woman helped Weston up. "Come to the bar and have a drink with me, so as to give this man space to ply his trade."

"I feel a bit guilty about not helping, but I suppose a glass of whiskey might assuage my shame."

"I hope you don't think me a supercilious heiress who considers cleaning floors beneath her—you know, figuratively. I just feel it's rude to presume to do another's work. After all, how would you feel if someone took over writing your Spinster stories?"

Weston motioned to the bartender. "A bourbon on the rocks for me and a…chardonnay, for the lady?"

"The lady will have a bourbon too," she said.

Weston smiled at the heiress as the bartender set to pouring the whiskey over ice. "So we know each other without ever having met."

The heiress took the glasses from the bartender and handed one to Weston. "I was up most of last night rereading *Saturnine Spinster*. Your work is very comforting…like literary mac and cheese."

"Thanks…and I'm sorry about your father."

"Losing someone slowly tricks you into thinking that when you finally lose them completely, you'll be ready for it. It's felt like I've been in a waking dream since yesterday, which must be why I'm not surprised to see you here, but tell me—how did you know my dad?"

"Truth be told, I didn't. I'm here helping out a friend who thinks someone in his company is up to no good, so I'm conducting a sort of informal inquiry."

"Oh." She sipped her drink.

"Do you know many of the people your father worked with?"

"I know them by sight, but not by motive. I knew almost nothing of Dad's business, so I couldn't say if any of them has ill intent."

"What's your line of work then?"

She pushed an errant tress of gray hair from her forehead back to her otherwise well-coiffed raven curls. "I write poetry."

"Ah, a poetess and an heiress."

"I imagine you can guess which pays my bills."

"What kind of poetry do you write?"

"The kind that people don't read."

"I've dabbled in that type of writing myself."

"Do you ever feel stuck writing the same character over and over?" she asked.

"Sure…sometimes."

"How do you get unstuck?"

"If I had any talent for it, I might try writing poetry instead." Weston took a sip of his whiskey. "Fictional characters aren't so very different from real people.

You might think you know them inside and out, but if given the chance, sometimes they can still surprise you."

"By that logic, the person you know best might be the one capable of surprising you the most."

"Yes, I suppose so."

"Then you may want to talk with that bald man walking toward the fountain. He was my dad's right-hand man…at least when he was still running the company. Dad trusted him implicitly, but I never liked the way he looked at me." She set her half-finished drink back on the bar. "I should go press the flesh. It's what Dad would've wanted, but I wish you luck with your inquiry, Mr. Payley."

****

H.P. watched the fountain lights transition, changing the effervescing water from shades of blue to green to yellow and back again.

"Mesmerizing, isn't it?"

It must be, H.P. thought, since he hadn't noticed the bald man who'd sidled up next to him. "Yes, very calming."

"This fountain used to have koi when it was first installed, but then the fish started dying. Turns out it was copper poisoning from the coins that visitors would toss in. Nothing ruins the tranquility of a water feature quite like a bunch of carp floating upside down. Hired a guy with a bucket to get rid of them, though I'm not sure how he disposed of the fish…too big to flush down the toilet."

H.P. frowned. "Sort of an inappropriate thought to share with a stranger at an event to honor a recently departed man."

"I don't know, I thought it appropriate since I figure you're here for more of a fishing trip than to pay your final respects." The man smiled a saurian grin. "Besides H.P., despite having never met, I don't consider you a stranger. I feel as if I know all about you."

"Are you a fan of my work?"

"Who has time to read anymore…though I was recently informed that the reading you gave earlier today was rather entertaining."

A young woman approached the pair. "Sir, they'd like you to say a few words to everyone up at the front, if you don't mind."

"Not at all." The bald man looked back at H.P. before following the woman. "Off to eulogize the dearly departed…but do enjoy the hors d'oeuvre. One never knows if it'll be your last meal."

H.P. shook his head. "You need to work on your pronoun-antecedent agreement."

Weston arrived at the fountain just as the bald man left. "I think that might be the guy who's behind all this."

"I'm pretty sure it is, and I have a feeling we're next on his hit list."

"How come?"

"I corrected his grammar."

Weston nodded. "Yeah, people really hate when you do that."

Chapter 40

Mr. Snide piloted the rickety pickup toward the state line, lamenting that they had to get back on the interstate in order to stay in email contact with the association, since the old truck was barely capable of highway speeds. Mr. Whip intently read the screen of his laptop in the passenger's seat. "We just got a new message…seems the client now wants us to acquire the two writers as well as Edwin."

"Just when I thought this job couldn't possibly get more ricockulous. Any brilliant recommendations on how to take all three of them, since they're undoubtedly on high alert and well protected?"

"Give me a sec…the encryption lag is worse than usual. Ah, according to the Egghead, the two writers just confronted him at a work function and are likely on their way home."

"They really get around," said Mr. Snide.

"They didn't have to spend the better part of the afternoon trying to find new transportation in the middle of nowhere."

"I take it you apprised the association of our status…I hope they're not suggesting that we try to intercept them en route with this jalopy?"

"Hang on…there's another message coming through. Based on the data they have, they suggest an alternative target and then offering up a trade.

Mr. Snide frowned. "What target?"

"A local target. How far are we away from Weston's hometown?"

"We're about twenty minutes out…so in this heap, we'll probably get there in a half hour."

"That should give us enough time."

Chapter 41

As he drove toward home, Weston handed his cellphone to H.P. in the passenger's seat. "Can you call Becca for me?"

"Sure, do you want me to hold the phone up to your ear?"

"No, just put her on speaker."

"Won't that make her mad?"

"What I have to tell her is going to make her mad regardless, but I'm hoping that if she knows three other people can hear her on speakerphone it'll keep her from hurling too many epithets."

Weston sighed as the phone rang.

"Weston, where the hell are you?"

"Hey Becca, my darl—"

"Stop talking and answer my question."

"I can't really answer your question if you won't let me talk."

"Listen, a cop Slim sent to my work to check on me, oh, happened to mention that you were chased and almost run off the road after your reading, so don't get cute with me you son of a—"

"Whoa Becca, I should inform you that you're on speakerphone in my car with Ed, Slim, and H.P."

"I don't care if you're in your car with the holy trinity. Why the hell are you still driving around and not at home?"

"You see, after the incident the officer mentioned—and frankly that cop shouldn't have spoken out of turn—we figured it'd be a good idea to try to identify the person we thought might be responsible for all this, though don't worry…we were under police surveillance the entire time."

"I'm not worried—I'm angry that you're not hunkered down someplace safe…so did you find this person?"

"We think so."

"We're pretty sure," added H.P.

"So he's in custody then, right?" asked Becky.

"Well now, Miss Becky," Slim began, "we can't just go around arresting whoever we please without probable cause, but I can assure you this individual is now being monitored at all times by the local authorities."

Becky took a deep breath. "But this guy was never the one actually doing all this shit—"

"Mom," said Lance's voice in the background, "S-word."

"Sorry hon…okay, I mean all this stuff—just the guy calling the shots, right?"

"That was my thinking," said Edwin.

Weston glared at Edwin in the rearview mirror. "So that's our concern—and it's a pretty mild concern—that even though we think we know who and where this guy is…he might still be able to get word out on some backchannel and order his henchmen to go after those closest to us since he probably knows we're on to him now, so out of an abundance of caution—"

"Stop abundantly cautioning me and tell me what you're going to do."

"We're about ninety minutes from home," said Weston, "so we'll be there in an hour. Where are you and the kids right now?"

"Lance and I just picked up Vancy from a 4-H event, and we're almost to my sister's place to get our daughter."

"Good, get Kim too and then drive straight to the house. Slim already has an officer there waiting for you. We'll be there as soon as we can, but don't worry darling."

"I already told you, I'm not worried—I'm angry."

"I'm a little worried," said Vance's voice.

Chapter 42

Becky pulled her Jeep into Kim's driveway and parked behind an old, beat-up truck. *Looks like my sister has a new boyfriend*, she thought, *and judging by the condition of his pickup, this one doesn't have a job either*.

"Mom, can we come inside?" asked Lance from the backseat.

"No, stay here—I'll just be a minute." Becky exited the Jeep and climbed the front steps to her sister's house. She opened the door to find Kim, who appeared anxious, seated on the couch holding Ance tightly.

"Please come in and sit down." Mr. Snide stepped from behind the door. "Forgive me, is it Ms. Hernandez or Mrs. Payley? Our information may not be up-to-date in that respect."

Becky stepped into the living room and took a seat on the couch next to her sister. "I go by Mrs. Payley in social settings but Ms. Hernandez at work."

Mr. Whip ducked into the room from the kitchen. "As you appear to already be aware, Ms. Hernandez, this isn't a social visit."

Becky caressed Ance's cheek to keep her calm. "What do you want?"

"Foremost what we want is for no one to get hurt," Mr. Snide answered. "However, what our client wants is your husband and his friends Edwin and H.P."

"I don't know where they are."

"We have a good idea of where they are," replied Mr. Whip, "likely headed downstate from Chicago to here."

Kim trembled. "So why don't you go get them?"

"It would be easier if they came to us." Mr. Snide peered out the window at Becky's Jeep. "We propose a trade, Ms. Hernandez—you and your two boys for the three we want."

Mr. Whip cleared his throat. "Shouldn't we take her sister and the baby too—five for three?"

Mr. Snide shook his head. "Unless we tie someone up in the bed of the truck, which wouldn't be very inconspicuous, we'd have a difficult time driving the seven of us around in two vehicles—one of which offers but a single row of seating. Besides, I'm opposed to taking a baby…both due to moral and practical considerations, and we can't very well leave the baby here by herself."

"That makes sense, but what do we do with her?" Mr. Whip pointed his gun at Kim.

"Take her phone, her car keys, and lock her in the basement with the kid."

Mr. Whip nodded. "All right."

"Now Ms. Hernandez, let's go have a talk with your boys—and the calmer you are, the calmer they'll be."

Becky stood apprehensively. "Calm, like Cheech and Chong."

Mr. Snide smiled. "It seems your years as a drug counselor have taken a toke."

Chapter 43

Weston took the exit ramp off the interstate. "Can you call Becca again to see if she wants us to grab dinner or if they've already eaten?"

H.P. picked up the cellphone. "Sure."

Edwin leaned forward. "Even if they have, we're still going to get something for ourselves, right?"

Weston glanced in the rearview mirror. "Don't fret, I won't let you starve, though I might be doing you a favor if I didn't let you order any dessert."

"There's that new barbecue joint on Stony Creek road that's mighty tasty," said Slim.

Weston shook his head. "Ed doesn't eat meat."

"They have hushpuppies."

Edwin turned to Slim. "I also don't eat foods named for animals...I know, it's weird."

"Huh, so you don't eat elephant ears either?"

"Nope."

"Or monkey bread?"

"Uh-uh."

"What about buzzard puke?"

"I'm fairly certain you made that one up, but for multiple reasons—no."

H.P. returned the mobile phone to the cupholder. "Becky's not answering."

"Maybe she's chasing one of the kids around the house or is otherwise occupied," Weston replied.

160

"I'll call the officer parked in her driveway and have him go check on the supper situation." Slim dialed a number on his cellphone. "Slim here. We're almost to you, but we wanted to know if…" Slim tilted his head back. "I texted you an hour ago that they should be there in a few minutes. Why didn't you call to tell me they ain't been home yet?"

Weston took his phone from the cupholder and handed it to H.P. "Can you call Kim? She's in my contacts under That Sister."

"No, I don't want you to go find them. Stay put and let me know if they show up." Slim ended the call. "If you don't get an answer at Kim's, I'll call the station and have all the on-duty officers start looking for Becky's Jeep."

H.P. lowered the cellphone from his ear. "It went straight to voicemail, like her phone is turned off."

"Seems unlikely, since she's usually on that thing day and night." Weston took a left turn. "We'll go to her place first."

Chapter 44

Weston slid to a stop in Kim's driveway and exited his car without turning off the engine.

Slim got out almost as fast. "Hang on, let me go first." Slim drew his sidearm and cautiously approached the house's open front door. "Police…come on out."

"We're trapped in the basement," yelled a panicked voice from within.

Slim entered the residence, crossed the living room into the kitchen, and stopped in front of the basement door, which was blocked by a refrigerator. "Hang on, Kim, we'll have you out in a minute." Slim pushed on the old-fashioned fridge, budging it slightly.

Entering the kitchen, Weston pulled from the other side. "These antiquated models aren't as easy to slide as the newer ones."

Slim leaned into it. "It must've taken a country hoss to move this thing all the way over here."

With considerable effort, the two managed to slide the refrigerator past the door frame. Weston swung open the basement door, and Kim emerged holding his daughter. "Pa da."

Weston kissed her forehead. "That's right, sweetie."

"They took Becky and the boys," said Kim.

"Do you know where?" asked Weston.

"Yeah, they told me to tell you that they'd

162

exchange the three of them for you, H.P., and Ed—tonight, at the old shooting club."

Slim crossed his arms. "And let me guess, they also told you to say that them three had better come alone."

Chapter 45

Weston skidded on a frozen puddle and turned onto a lane that ran along a barbed wire fence, which led to the shooting club tucked away in the distant darkness. "You know, none of you have to come with me. These are my people."

H.P. turned to Weston. "They're our people too."

"And Kate can't come home until we finish this," Edwin added from the backseat.

Mayor McCormick leaned forward. "Besides, you risked your neck for my boy, so it's only fair that I do likewise for yours."

"All right...thanks." Weston drove down the shadowy lane. Soon his headlights found the gatehouse, which was burned-out and missing its gate. "Doesn't look like we're the first ones who've been back here since this place closed down." They continued on toward the main house, whose windows had been covered with plywood, which in turn had been covered by graffiti. Despite the loud-colored spray paint that adorned the abandoned structure, the surroundings were eerily quiet.

Weston parked under the *porte cochère*. "Last time I was here, there was a valet to greet me."

A pair of headlights illuminated a swath of the field past the mansion, and a vehicle slowly approached.

"I think that's our welcoming committee," said

H.P.

An old truck came to a stop in front of Weston's car. Its headlights went dark, revealing a single occupant in the cab of the pickup and three people sitting in the bed. The driver got out. "I left clear instructions that only three should come...I count four."

Weston moved to get out, but the mayor put a hand on his shoulder. "Let me talk to him first." The mayor exited the sedan. "My name is McCormick. I'm the town's mayor and family friend of the people you've taken. I've come along to make sure no one gets hurt."

"You're outside your jurisdiction, Mr. Mayor," replied Mr. Snide.

"Nonetheless, I can assure you that if you turn over the three you have there and let us all leave in peace, I'll delay my reporting of this incident to the county and state authorities until tomorrow. You can be well on your way by then."

"I could've been well on my way at any time I chose. Do you really think that a compelling offer?"

The mayor took a step forward. "Frankly no, but I thought it worth a try...politicians are optimists by nature."

"Funny, I always figured you were cynics."

"We are that too at times, which might be the reason we're so often thought of as hypocritical."

"So then why did you really come, Mr. Mayor?"

"The cynical part of me was concerned that the three you have wouldn't be in a condition to drive themselves away from here."

"I'm not in the business of harming women and children, Mr. Mayor."

"Who you callin' a child, chump?" Vance's voice

shouted from the bed of the truck.

"Though I admit that I'm starting to lose my patience with the teenager."

Mayor McCormick nodded. "Yeah, they can be mouthy."

Mr. Snide moved to the back of the pickup and lowered the tailgate. "As you see, they're all unharmed. In fact, their condition is such that you won't need to drive them at all...the four of you will be leaving here on foot. Tell the other three to get out of the car and to put their cellphones and keys on the hood of this truck."

Weston, Edwin, and H.P. exited the sedan and emptied their pockets as Mr. Snide unlocked the chain that bound Becky and her boys. Mr. Snide collected the phones and keys as Weston hugged Becky. "No matter what happens to me, I'll always be with you, my Becca."

"I don't want your pledges," Becky replied. "I just want you."

Weston turned to an angry Van and a frightened Lance. "Listen, I know there's a lot to process right now, but I need you two to focus on looking after your mom and sister. I'm not sure what's going to happen to us, but whatever it is, I'll be okay with it so long as I know you all are safe. Promise me that you'll both take care of the two most important girls in my life...and the two most important boys. Can you promise that?"

"I promise," Lance answered.

Van nodded. "Me too...we'll be all right—but do whatever you can to be the same. Someday I might want you as my best man too."

Chapter 46

Slim watched from the woods near the entrance to the underground shooting range as the old pickup drove around the far side of the pond, heading away from him. He cursed to himself and pulled his cellphone from his pocket. First he tried Mayor McCormick's number, but the call went directly to voicemail. Then he called Weston's phone and again got sent straight to voicemail. He cursed once more as he raced through the trees toward his truck parked along an unpaved access road.

When Slim reached his truck, he quickly climbed inside and turned the key in the ignition. Nothing happened. He pounded the steering wheel with his fists and cursed again. Then he popped the hood and got out. As he raised the hood with a creak, he felt the barrel of a pistol press against the back of his skull. "Damnit."

"You certainly swear a lot," said Mr. Whip.

"It's been a trying day."

"I doubt tonight's going to get any easier." Mr. Whip took a step back. "I disconnected the battery. Go ahead and reconnect it."

Slim reaffixed the cable to the battery terminal and closed the hood. "It ain't nice to mess with a man's truck."

"I'm not in the business of being nice, though I tell you what—I'll let you drive it one last time, but first you've got to take off your boots."

"What for?"

"Don't 'what for' me," Mr. Whip said. "You're not wearing a holster, which means you most likely have a gun stuffed down in your boots."

Slim frowned as he pulled off his boots.

"Now turn them over."

Slim did as instructed, and a snub-nosed revolver fell out of his bootleg. Mr. Whip smiled. "Okay, kick it over to me."

Again, Slim did as he was told. Mr. Whip knelt to pick up the revolver and then threw it into the woods.

"My daddy gave me that gun." Slim shook his head. "Can I at least put my boots back on?"

"Sure, go ahead." Mr. Whip walked around to the passenger's side as he motioned with his pistol across the hood for Slim to get into the driver's seat. Once inside the cab, with his gun still trained on Slim, Mr. Whip put on his seat belt. Slim started to do likewise. "Don't bother."

"But it's the law."

"You're taking the night off, lawman. I don't want you crashing us into a tree or running us into a ditch, hoping that I'll come out of it worse than you. For good measure, I also tossed that two-way radio you had stashed under the seat into the woods, so don't get any ideas."

"I need one idea…where am I driving to?" Slim started up his truck. "Not much is open this time of night."

"I know just the spot…Edwin Hubert's old telescope."

"For an out-of-towner you seem to know this area

pretty good."

"We do our due diligence. I recently read the reports from some associates of mine that you and your friends have run afoul of in the past, which is why I figured you'd think we were taking the other three out to that retired underground lab."

"That's what we thought all right." Slim pulled onto the access road. "None of us even considered that you'd have any interest in a burned-down telescope."

"Setting a fire someplace that's already burnt is a good way to get rid of evidence."

"Arson's real big with you guys, ain't it? And when you say 'evidence,' you mean people, right?"

"As a professional courtesy, I promise not to let you or your friends burn to death."

"That's mighty big of you, big man, but then that ain't quite the same as saying you're not gonna burn our bodies at some point."

"Just drive the truck, cowboy."

Chapter 47

Mr. Snide parked in front of the KEEP OUT sign that dangled across the dark road. He exited the cab of the pickup and began unlocking the padlocks that kept Weston, Edwin, and H.P. chained inside the bed of the truck.

"I haven't been out here in months," said Edwin.

H.P. sniffed at the air. "It still smells like smoke."

Weston looked over at Mr. Snide. "It never occurred to me that you'd bring us out here."

Mr. Snide nodded. "That's what we sort of figured."

"We?" asked H.P.

"The inverterate honesty of politicians notwithstanding, we thought it unlikely that you'd be unaccompanied, so while I chatted with your mayor and facilitated the exchange, my partner was on the lookout for interlopers. He texted on the way over that he caught your cop friend prowling around in the woods at the shooting range. They should be here soon." Mr. Snide unlocked the chain that bound their feet and lowered the tailgate. "Okay fellas, hop on out."

The three stood unsteadily. "Any chance you'd be so kind as to undo the chains threaded through our beltloops?" asked Edwin.

"None whatsoever," answered Mr. Snide. "I'm not chasing you three through the woods. Now come on down, and don't be concerned about falling. I doubt they'll be the only bumps and bruises you get tonight."

The three tentatively stepped from the edge of the tailgate together—Weston and H.P. landing on their feet, with Edwin crumpling to the ground between them, causing the other two to topple over on top of him. The three struggled to regain their feet for a time. Finally, Mr. Snide helped Edwin to stand, which allowed the other two to right themselves.

Weston took a deep breath. "You know, the last time we were duct taped."

"So I read in the report," replied Mr. Snide. "Em always preferred the compactness of duct tape to rope or chain. The problem is that once taped, it becomes almost impossible to move the prisoner. I prefer chain to rope myself, since constantly tying and untying knots gets tedious."

"Why do you call her Em?" asked H.P.

"It's short for Emerald. She had a thing for green-themed names. I don't know the real names of any of my associates."

"We knew her real name," said H.P.

"Huh, perhaps that'll be one of the things we chat about later."

Weston exhaled. "I don't suppose an unsigned note from your client stating that they'd never bother us again would help our cause?"

Mr. Snide chuckled. "Do you happen to have the note on you?"

"No, but if you let me go, I could get it and be back within the hour."

"I don't think so."

Chapter 48

Weston, Edwin, and H.P. sat chained together around the campfire Mr. Snide had built near the charred remnants of the radio telescope's housing. Mr. Snide returned with another armful of wood and threw a couple more logs on the fire. Then he warmed his hands above the flames that licked at the gelid night air as he looked skyward to behold the firmament. "I've got to hand it to you Edwin, this really is a great spot for stargazing."

"Yes, I always thought so."

A twig snapped in the woods. Mr. Snide turned to see Slim and Mr. Whip step into the clearing. "Nice night for a fire."

"Most nights are," replied Mr. Snide.

Mr. Whip led Slim over to the others and chained them together. "I didn't miss any good ghost stories, did I?"

Weston smiled at Slim. "Nope, but we're planning to have s'mores soon."

Mr. Whip moved to the other side of the fire next to Mr. Snide. "Any word from the Egghead?"

"The association emailed to let us know he's on his way," Mr. Whip whispered.

"I thought he'd been under surveillance since meeting H.P. this afternoon...that his house's alarm status was being monitored."

"It seems he was able to sneak down his study's balcony without turning off his alarm—the same way we got in. He had a taxi waiting on the next block that took him to a car-rental agency where he used the association's dummy account to rent a vehicle."

"The Egghead's more resourceful than I gave him credit for."

Mr. Whip nodded. "It would appear so."

"Then we're supposed to babysit these four until he gets here? Perhaps we really should've brought some snacks."

"Maybe so…after last time, he wants to interrogate Edwin personally."

"What about the others?"

"No mention of the cop, but apparently the Egghead has a score to settle with the two writers, though I get the sense that his people aren't supportive of that play."

"What makes you think that?" asked Mr. Snide.

"Just a hunch."

****

On the other side of the crackling campfire, H.P. furtively kicked Weston's shin to get his attention. "Does the tall guy look familiar to you?"

Weston stared across the fire. "Yeah, through the flames he kind of reminds me of bigfoot, sans face paint and fur."

H.P. shook his head. "It was a ghillie suit."

"What the hell are you boys whispering about?" Slim asked.

"I think maybe we've met your escort before," Weston answered.

Chapter 49

The Egghead drove his rental car past the darkened fields that stretched endlessly along the interstate. His cellphone buzzed in the passenger's seat—its screen illuminating the sedan's interior. He glanced at his phone and saw that Zeta Dry Cleaners was calling. He tapped the screen. "You're on speakerphone, but it's just me in the car."

"This is the moderator, and you're on speakerphone too—with a virtual meeting room full of council members, all of whom had different plans for tonight."

"There was no reason to assemble the committee on my account."

"I beg to differ. I took a temperature check just before I dialed your number. Half of us applaud the initiative you've shown, and the other half think you're overstepping, but all of us are concerned."

"There's no cause for concern," the Egghead replied.

A new voice spoke up. "FYI—saying things like 'there's no cause for concern' during an emergent situation that could jeopardize our entire operation is concerning."

The Egghead took a deep breath. "Allow me to rephrase…there's no cause for anxiety. The situation is well in hand. I just spoke to my association contact, and their team has Edwin as well as the two novelists at a secure location, which I'm on my way to now."

"What are your intentions once you arrive?" asked a female voice.

"To compel Edwin to reveal Kate's location, of course."

"You do realize that if she divulges to the proper authorities the data she's been privy to over the past few months, it could implicate this entire council, right?" asked the moderator.

"I understand."

"I don't think that you do," said the female voice. "I was one of those who opposed providing her with so much access to sensitive information, despite your assurances that you'd disaggregated the data to such an extent she couldn't possibly connect all the pieces."

"Kate's the best mind in this field that we had available to us," replied the Egghead. "Her input saved us incalculable time, preventing us from pursuing dead-ends as well as alerting us to possibilities that no one else recognized."

"And now we can't find her," the female voice said. "If she surfaces, and the investigatory agencies who've been watching our members, waiting for us to make a mistake, get to her first…well, we'll have given them exactly what they need to take direct action against us. I told this committee she was too high a risk, and then when she made overtures of blowing the whistle, I told you to simply have her eliminated posthaste."

The Egghead cleared his throat. "I admit that was an error in judgement on my part…one which I intend to remedy."

"How?" she asked.

"The serum my private laboratory has been working on is finally finished. I plan to cram it down that fat man's gullet and wait for her whereabouts to come spewing out."

"Does that course of action allay your concerns?" asked the moderator.

"It does," the female voice answered.

"What of the two writers?" another voice asked.

"I'd thought we'd settled that matter months ago," said a new voice. "Even together they don't know enough to pose a significant threat to us."

"Yes," replied the moderator, "but now they've turned up yet again—like proverbial bad pennies."

"Then, when the information we need has been extracted, just do away with them," the female voice said. "All of them."

The Egghead grinned. "For once, you and I are in complete agreement."

"So it's decided," said the moderator. "However, there is one final item. I've been monitoring the daily reports from the association closely, and the older of the two associates assigned to this undertaking has of late exhibited behavior that is…'disquieting' I believe is how it was characterized. Based on your brief interactions with the pair, do you concur?"

"I do indeed," the Egghead answered.

"I'll inform the association coordinator then. As luck would have it, the other assigned associate is something of a hyphenate within their organization, doubling as he sometimes does as a dispatcher of wayward associates. I suspect, once the job is completed, that they'll instruct him to permanently terminate his partner's affiliation with the association."

Chapter 50

Edwin and H.P. gazed at the night sky, as Weston and Slim watched the dancing flames. "You ain't got a harmonica on you, by chance?"

Mr. Snide looked down at Slim from across the fire. "No, but my associate happens to be an excellent yodeler."

"Is that right?"

"You should ask him about it when he gets back…it's an amusing story."

"Where did your partner get off to anyway?" asked Weston.

"I don't suppose he drove into town for a couple of pizzas," said Edwin.

"I'm feeling a bit peckish myself, but regrettably no. He's driving around, trying to get a signal so he can report in with our association. This situation has come under enhanced scrutiny, which means they think they're entitled to constant updates."

"We all know how that can be…just let me do my damn job that you hired me to do." Slim looked over at Weston, Edwin, and H.P. "Oh right, I sometimes forget you boys ain't got real jobs with bosses and such."

"So what's the yodeling story?" asked H.P.

"You should wait for him to tell it…I wouldn't do it justice." Mr. Snide rubbed his hands together over the fire. "I read that in addition to being a novelist you also teach creative writing."

"That's right…writing doesn't pay what it used to."

"More's the pity," replied Mr. Snide. "You know, I'm something of a novelist manqué."

"What's a manqué?" asked Slim.

"An animal that throws its own feces," Weston answered.

Mr. Snide laughed. "I never threw it, but I certainly wrote it…about a hundred pages worth."

"What was it about?" H.P. asked.

"This delivery driver who was nearly retired. He'd make the same delivery every day to a remote sushi restaurant outside the city that received a daily shipment of seafood. He drove slower than most of the other drivers, which is why his company had him take the one faraway delivery that took up most of the day, but eventually he got so old that he could no longer unload the fish when he arrived at the restaurant, so they assigned him a partner…a young guy who was strong but too impatient to drive, though he was great at toting fish, so they made a good team. The young man looked up to the older driver, because being his teammate gave him purpose, imbued him with a sense of value he'd never felt before. His childhood had been challenging—didn't do well in school…there was a whole backstory. Anyway, the two would talk during their day-long drives; the youngster would ask him questions—simple questions mostly that he'd be too embarrassed to ask anyone else for fear that they might laugh and think him stupid. The old man always concluded his thoughtful answers with comforting phrase, like 'buck up, copilot' and 'tomorrow's another delivery.'"

H.P. nodded. "That's not a bad beginning."

"So where'd the story go?" Weston asked. "Besides back and forth to the sushi restaurant."

"That's just it," said Mr. Snide. "I didn't have a clue. I thought it a decent enough premise for a story, but then after about the third delivery I realized something was missing."

"An ending?" asked Edwin.

Mr. Snide shook his head. "More like a plot, I'd say. I had all these different ideas for the things the two would talk about, but nothing ever came from it. I thought if I wrote a few dozen pages the story would sort of reveal itself."

"But it didn't," said Weston. "Yeah, I've been there."

"Writing is all about making decisions," added H.P. "Sometimes those decisions lead to driving on a road to nowhere."

Mr. Whip stepped out of the woods. "Funny, that's where I just got back from."

Mr. Snide turned to Mr. Whip as he approached the fire. "Were you able to get in touch with the association?"

"Yes, I communicated directly with the coordinator. It seems he just had a confab with the moderator who presides over the entire client council. Directions to get here have been relayed to the Egghead, so he should be joining us soon."

Chapter 51

After following the tortuous directions he'd been given, the Egghead parked behind two pickup trucks on a dark road lined by trees. He walked through the woods as instructed, and to his mild surprise did indeed happen upon a massive, burned-out radio telescope set in a clearing. He followed the sound of voices and the glow of a fire.

"It's not often that we're joined by a client out in the field," said Mr. Snide.

The Egghead pointed to Weston and H.P. across the fire. "These two made my direct involvement necessary."

"The coordinator mentioned that you had a plan for extracting the information you require from Edwin," Mr. Whip said.

"That's right." The Egghead reached his right hand into his coat pocket and pulled out a couple of candy bars. "Though I imagine it'll be a grueling process, so I bought a few snacks when I stopped for gas, if you want a pick-me-up before we get started."

Mr. Whip and Mr. Snide each took a chocolate bar.

Edwin watched as they peeled away the wrappers. "I don't suppose you brought enough for the whole class."

The Egghead reached into his left coat pocket to reveal a third candy bar. "Sorry, no…just three for the teachers." He stepped around the fire toward Edwin. "You know what, I also grabbed some drive-thru on the way down. I was saving this as my dessert, but I'm not really all that hungry. You can have it, Ed. We didn't know each other well, but I always held you in high esteem. It's a Milky Way."

Edwin reached up his chained wrists and hesitantly accepted the chocolate bar. "Given the circumstances, you'll excuse me if I don't say thank you."

"Of course."

Edwin unwrapped the candy bar. "You three want to split this with me?"

"No thanks," Weston answered. "I had a bite to eat earlier at the memorial service."

H.P. nodded. "Me too."

"Go ahead," said Slim.

Edwin voraciously consumed the chocolate as the Egghead warmed his hands in his pockets and returned to the other side of the fire.

Mr. Whip dropped his candy bar wrapper into the flames. "So for Edwin's interrogation, are you thinking that we'll take him out behind the woodshed, so to speak?"

"No, that's much too crude a method for a man of his intellect." The Egghead pulled an eyeglass case from his left pocket and opened the clamshell container to reveal a syringe.

Edwin eyed the syringe as he licked his fingertips. "Sodium thiopental? While barbiturates suppress higher cortical brain function and inhibition, their efficacy for this type of application is dubious. Besides, I don't like needles."

The Egghead grinned. "Oh, it's not a barbiturate.

It's a designer cocktail containing norepinephrine, melatonin, GABA, and histamine…as well as few other chemicals that I had my personal laboratorians create, which we haven't bothered to name yet. This amnesic effectively causes a condition of nearly instantaneous sleep deprivation to such a degree that the subject enters into a peculiar state of mania, during which one simply loses all sense of reality. You'll no longer be able to comprehend your circumstances or even understand the very concept of truth…let alone have the wherewithal to lie. And as it happens, the serum is just as effective if taken orally, so this syringe isn't for injecting you. It's for injecting the chocolate bar you just ate."

Edwin lurched forward and heaved. The Egghead set the syringe back in its case, snapping it shut and returning it to his coat pocket. "You can attempt to cough up the chocolate if you like, but then I'll just have these two hold you down, and I'll inject what's left directly into your bloodstream. Besides, the serum was formulated to be fast acting, so it's most likely already begun to take hold."

Edwin sat up straight again, wobbling slightly in the process. Then his eyelids twitched as if in REM sleep.

"Ed, can you hear me?" Weston watched as his friend slumped to the side and fell to the ground. "What will it do to him?"

"I'm rather curious about that myself," replied the Egghead. "As you might imagine, drugs like these don't get human trials…at least not here in the States. Most of our lab rats eventually slept off the effects, though I don't anticipate he'll get that chance."

"Should I unchain him?" asked Mr. Whip.

The Egghead nodded. "Yes, he should very soon enter into a trance-like consciousness, so we'll move him away from the others to prevent distractions while your partner remains here to keep an eye on these three."

Chapter 52

Edwin's head rolled back and forth as Mr. Whip held him up against a tree. The Egghead slapped Edwin across the face. "Time to have that talk. What's your name?"

Edwin opened his eyes. "Dr. Edwin Hubert."

"Where are you?"

Edwin looked from side to side. "In the woods it would appear."

"What about Kate…where is she?"

Edwin scanned his surroundings. "Not here."

The Egghead pressed the side of his hand against Edwin's trachea. "I don't know if some part of you is resisting, but there's no scenario in which you survive this, so you might as well make things easier for yourself. Now where is Kate?"

"Not here," Edwin struggled to answer.

"I think he's telling the truth," Mr. Whip said. "You're just not asking the right questions."

The Egghead took a step back. "Then by all means."

Mr. Whip turned Edwin's head toward him. "Is Kate in hiding?"

Edwin gasped for breath. "Yes."

"Where?"

"I don't know."

"So how would you contact her then if this were all

over…if it was safe for her to come home?"

"I would send her a message."

"And how would you do that?"

Edwin exhaled heavily. "I would take out a personal ad in a newspaper."

The Egghead stepped forward. "What paper?"

"The Danville News."

"Where is that located?"

"In Danville."

The Egghead pulled a folding knife from his pants pocket, flicked open the blade, and held it against Edwin's throat. "There are Danvilles all over this country…what state?"

Edwin blinked several times. "Alabama."

The Egghead lowered his knife. "Gotcha."

"Wait," said Mr. Whip, "I doubt it's that simple. Edwin, did you two have a safe word—some kind of phrase or code—so that she knew it was really you trying to contact her?"

Edwin blinked again. "Chi Omicron."

"Cute," said the Egghead.

"What does that mean?" asked Mr. Whip.

"Chi and Omicron are the Greek letters for X and O."

Chapter 53

When he noticed that he'd lost feeling in his toes, H.P. moved his feet closer to the fire.

Mr. Snide watched as he stretched out his legs. "Be careful. If your toes are frostbitten, heating them up too quickly could cause blistering."

"Somehow I don't think blisters will be my biggest problem tonight," replied H.P.

"No, I expect not," agreed Mr. Snide.

H.P. bent his knees again, retracting his feet slightly from the fire. "You know, I thought of an ending for your story…or at least the next chapter."

"Yeah, what's that?" asked Mr. Snide.

"It occurred to me that what you've written is the beginning of a classic everyman story. Your driver thinks he has made a life that he's perfectly suited for, so he's reluctant to try anything new. We all feel that way a little, especially as we get older. We've worked hard to get to a place in our career where we're comfortable…driving to the same destination day after day is easier than when we first started out on the job, and everything required learning."

Mr. Snide nodded. "Makes sense…so where does my character go from there?"

"Ultimately, that's up to you as the author, but first what he needs to do is quit his job. There's no arc to the story if your main character doesn't change, and he'll never change if he keeps doing the same thing over and over."

"That's a good point," said Mr. Snide. "I'll give it some thought."

"While you think about that, think about this," Weston said. "Does it make you nervous that your partner sometimes gets assigned to kill other associates? Em's real name was Allison Belched, and she was shot in the back of the head by your partner. He left her body in a blazing barn to burn."

Mr. Snide poked at the fire with a stick. "You may've known Em's real name, but what you don't know is if she had it coming."

"Oh, she definitely had it coming," Weston replied. "But how do you know you don't? Who in your organization decides whether one of your associates has it coming or not? Do your clients, like that bald jackass, get a say?"

Slim expectorated into the fire. "I sure as shit wouldn't want to partner up with somebody who'd fragged a fellow teammate."

Mr. Snide snapped his poking stick in two and dropped it into the fire. "I get what you three are trying to do—quite clever, even if it is somewhat ham-fisted. During my years in this job, I've seen people, like chrome dome, play the bad guy because they're convinced every story needs one, so why not be a key player rather than a minor character...other times it's just who they are." Mr. Snide turned his head toward the sound of footsteps. "I don't always like delivering fish, but I enjoy driving the truck."

"I knew there was more behind you always wanting to drive than just the coffee." Mr. Whip led a semi-conscious Edwin into the firelight and sat him down next to the other three. "They didn't give you any trouble, did they?"

"No," answered Mr. Snide. "We were just having a literary discussion."

"Sorry I missed it." Mr. Whip began to reconnect H.P.'s chains to Edwin's.

"Don't bother," said the Egghead. "He'll be completely unconscious soon."

Mr. Whip lightly pushed Edwin's shoulder, and he tipped backwards, lying flat on the ground. "It looks like he already is…good thing you got the information you needed when you did."

"Why are you doing all this?" asked H.P. "What can Kate possibly know that merits this level of heinousness? Just because you look like Lex Luthor doesn't mean you're required to try taking over the world."

The Egghead frowned. "I don't want to rule the world; I want to save it."

"Jesus, it's not the first time I've heard that from one of you people," said Weston. "It's like a disease with your kind."

"Again, you have it the wrong way around—curing disease is my aim. Kate was working on a vaccine that could've prevented a host of childhood diseases, which can be administered not through syringes but rather via mosquitos, allowing us to sidestep the entire anti-vaxxer moron-athon; however, I also had her looking at another vaccine…for a disease the human race has yet to encounter. She correctly deduced that this other vaccine was intended to combat a super-strain of malaria…that my lab developed."

"But why release a super-strain of malaria at the same time as a super-vaccine?" H.P. asked.

"No, you missed it." Weston shook his head. "He's going to release the super-strain and the super-vaccine, minus the vaccine for the new malaria."

"We've heard this ditty before," added Slim, "at least a variation of it."

Weston nodded. "I'll wager that's what was in the case taken from the train."

Mr. Snide turned toward the Egghead. "You told me the canister in the case contained vaccines."

"It wasn't a lie," replied the Egghead. "I just omitted mentioning that it also contained a little something extra."

H.P. tilted his head. "But why attempt to introduce a cure for many diseases only to propagate a new one?"

The Egghead smiled. "Attempt? It's been done…well, very nearly. We've learned from the recent pandemic that there's much more money to be made from vaccines for diseases that grab headlines than diseases that have plagued mankind for millennia. Even though millions are infected with malaria each year, and thousands of children die annually, it's not news simply because it's not new. But if a super-strain of malaria were to rear its head in the States rather than in sub-Saharan Africa…then that would be newsworthy, and if children started to get sick here the way they do in rural areas overseas, politicians would dislocate their arms trying to throw money at finding a cure."

"Which you'll have all set to go in your back pocket," said Weston.

"That's right, but our super-malaria vaccine, theoretically, should be able to eradicate all forms of malaria. The long-term goal is to exterminate the human race's oldest foe."

H.P. shook his head. "Funny, I thought mankind's oldest enemy was greed."

"Greed certainly plays a role," said the Egghead. "Developing vaccines isn't cheap, though they are considerably cheaper than what we charge once they're completed, but it's not all about money. Our models predict, within an acceptable margin of error, that the modified mosquitos will save more lives than they'll take."

Weston sighed. "And your mass-mosquito-vaccination campaign will turn down the noise around other diseases so that the public can focus its attention and tax dollars on your new super-strain of malaria."

The Egghead nodded. "Of course, but let's not make my motives out to be completely mercenary. I mean everyone—from children in Africa to future generations here—wins…in the long run. I, and my group, just also happen to benefit in the short term as well. Anyway, speaking of mercenaries, let's get this next part over with quickly. I have a funeral to attend in a few hours."

"How do you want it done?" asked Mr. Whip.

"Oh, I'm not particular," answered the Egghead. "Bullets in the brains are fine with me."

"You know, I was thinking about this situation," said Mr. Snide. "They have nothing on you…at least nothing that would constitute proof in a court of law, and since you snuck out of your house like a teenager going to a rock concert, the cops can't tie you to their abduction. Killing them would only draw attention to their cause. You got the information you need to eliminate the real threat. Why not cut them loose?"

Mr. Whip turned to his partner. "You let Edwin go before, didn't you?"

"No, not exactly. I didn't unlock his chains and open the door for him. I merely presented him with the opportunity to escape. He wasn't going to tell us anything useful, no matter how much we beat on him…he's not the type."

Mr. Whip shook his head. "That wasn't your call to make."

"But it was the right call," replied Mr. Snide. "When I got into this racket, it was mostly bad guys offing other bad guys, but these days…I mean Jesus, we're talking about an astronomer, a cop, and a couple of writers—and don't pretend that you don't recognize these two. I have it on good authority that you saved them once."

"Because those were my orders. Now we're being ordered to do the opposite, and I don't want to hear about any Tennessee poetry. We're soldiers—soldiers do as they're told."

"You're such a company man."

"Are you going to do your job or not?" asked the Egghead.

"I'm sorry fellas." Mr. Snide walked behind Slim, Weston, and H.P. "You heard me…I tried to talk them out of it. You never should've confronted chrome dome on his own turf the way you did—makes guys like him edgy and mean."

H.P. leaned forward. "But he came up to us…to me."

"Is that a fact?" Mr. Snide pulled his pistol from his waistband. "This snafu gets stupider by the minute."

"In your estimation, I think I'm about to make it stupider still," said the Egghead. "First, I want you to toss Edwin on the fire."

"What the hell are you talking about?" asked Mr. Snide.

"I'm curious about the serum's potential application as an anesthetic." The Egghead moved around the fire and stood between H.P. and Edwin. "And it occurs to me that this is a rare opportunity for a human test."

Mr. Snide pointed at Edwin. "What in the world will burning this man alive prove?"

"If he doesn't regain consciousness during his immolation, it'll prove the serum's potency as an anesthestic."

Mr. Whip leaned over to grab Edwin's ankles.

Mr. Snide turned to him. "And you're okay with this?"

"It's not my proudest moment, but nobody forced me to take this job." Mr. Whip dragged Edwin toward the fire. "We were going to burn them at some point anyway."

Distracted by their disagreement, H.P. took the opportunity to kick the Egghead in his kneecaps, causing him to reel backwards and fall into the fire. "Turnabout is fair play!"

Mr. Whip dropped Edwin's legs and lunged toward the Egghead, pulling him out of the fire by his coat front, the back of which was ablaze. Mr. Whip quickly stripped him of his coat, throwing it to the ground and stomping out the flames.

The Egghead struggled to catch his breath. "Shoot…them…now."

Mr. Whip pulled his pistol, but Mr. Snide grabbed his wrist before he could fire it. Mr. Whip struggled to raise his arm in order to break free of the grip. "You're a smart guy, but this is a dumb play. Hand-to-hand…I'm out of your league."

"You wouldn't be the first guy to mistake being bigger for being badder." Mr. Snide strained to keep hold of Mr. Whip's wrist. "Though I think it's time to even the odds." Mr. Snide stuck the muzzle of his gun in the crook of Mr. Whip's arm. A shot rang out. Mr. Snide still held Mr. Whip's forearm, but it was now severed at the elbow from his person. Mr. Whip fell violently to the ground.

Mr. Snide emptied his hands and swiftly took off his belt. He knelt next to Mr. Whip and tied a tourniquet around his bicep to stanch the flow of blood. "Sorry to disarm you, George."

"Sorry to stab you, Geoff."

Mr. Snide leaned back with a knife handle protruding from his chest—the blade buried deep. "I was trying to save you."

"Orders…from the association," Mr. Whip said as the life drained from his body. "I'm a good…soldier."

Certain that the two mercenaries were both dead or nearly so, the Egghead darted for the gun Mr. Snide had dropped near the fire, but Slim used the heel of his boot to pull Mr. Whip's pistol close, snatching it up and taking aim. "I'd leave that right there, if I was you."

Seeing that Slim had the drop on him, the Egghead kicked at the fire, scattering sparks and embers in their direction—using the fiery distraction to make his escape into the woods. The three used their cupped hands to throw dirt on the burning debris that surrounded them in order to extinguish the flames. Then the trio turned their attention to Mr. Snide.

"The hor…the hor…" Mr. Snide attempted to say with his final breath.

"The horror?" asked H.P. "Like from Conrad's *Heart of Darkness*?"

"No…the…horse."

"I think he means the stallion that Edwin mentioned," said Weston. "That must be where he injected the super-strain."

Mr. Snide nodded slowly before falling over dead. Weston turned from Mr. Snide to Mr. Whip as the pool of blood around his pale body soaked into the ground. "I guess we're not going to get to hear that yodeling anecdote after all."

Slim looked at Weston and H.P. "No offense, but this is the last time I go camping with you boys."

Chapter 54

After much scooting and contorting, the three managed to maneuver themselves close enough to Mr. Snide to retrieve the padlock keys from his pocket. Once the chains that bound them were unlocked, each stood to stretch their legs and arms.

"I don't see how guys on a chain gang can stand that all day long," said H.P.

Slim picked up the other pistol off the ground. "They ain't there by choice."

"Beats a night in the box." Weston turned to H.P. "By the way, the Pirate Hunter would've been proud of your little move back there."

"Yeah, I'm going to miss that guy," said H.P.

"Miss him?" Weston kneeled next to Edwin to feel for a pulse.

"All that talk about driving to nowhere got me thinking that I need to make a change myself." H.P. shook the dirt and ash from the Egghead's partially burnt coat. "In order to grow, I think it's time I say goodbye to the Pirate Hunter…at least for a while."

"How's Ed looking?" asked Slim.

"Like he's going to sleep for a week," answered Weston.

"Let him be then." Slim examined the pistol. "I'll go get a blanket from my truck, and we can rig up a stretcher to move him."

"I'll go with you in case chrome dome is still lurking about," said Weston.

H.P. covered Edwin's torso with the coat. "I'll stay here with Ed then."

Slim walked toward the woods. "Just holler if you need anything, and we'll come running."

"That's right." Weston jogged to catch up. "Slim, how about you give me that other gun."

"Oh, I didn't realize you'd gotten your carrier's permit."

"No, Becca won't let me have a gun in the house."

"Smart lady."

"Come on, you saw how well I handled that gun at the underground shooting range."

"You mean when you got your damn toe blown off?" asked Slim.

"Don't act like you've never been shot before."

"I never tried to jump on somebody that was aiming to shoot me."

The two walked out of the woods onto the road near the "KEEP OUT" sign. Slim eyed the flat tires of the beat-up truck and then those of his own pickup. "That motherless son of a bitch slashed my tires."

"You know he can't be both, right?" Weston looked inside the beater. "At least our phones are still here."

"That's something I guess, though I reckon we'll have to do a fair bit of walking before we can get a signal."

"Then I'll take that blanket back to H.P. and let him know."

Chapter 55

The Egghead sat in his customary booth at the café he went to most every morning. He ate his usual breakfast, a Denver omelet with a side of Canadian bacon, but something felt different today. He thought perhaps that wearing a suit and tie had him out of sorts…or more likely he felt off because he got no sleep the night before, barely having had enough time to drive home and shower off the campfire smell before getting dressed. He peeked through the venetian blinds and saw the same dark-blue sedan that had been parked across the cul-de-sac from his house last night. *That must be it. But what's to worry about? The cops don't have anything on me. Soon they'll lose interest and go chase after some other wild goose.*

As the Egghead finished his eggs, H.P., redolent of smoke, slid onto the booth cushion on the other side of the table. The Egghead considered bolting for the door, but once again it occurred to him, *They've got nothing, so there's nothing to be worried about.* "The table's all yours if you want it. I was just leaving."

"I thought we could have a quick chat first," said H.P.

"I don't think so. I'm on my way to a funeral."

The Egghead moved to leave the booth, but Slim sat down next to him, blocking his exit. "This won't take long, and then we can arrange a police escort, if you like."

The Egghead drank the last of his coffee. "Listen, fellas...I think you've got the wrong guy. I don't know who you are—"

H.P. shook his head. "I'm hurt...we just met yesterday."

The Egghead nodded vaguely. "Oh, that's right...at the memorial service at work for my boss. You're that writer who had no business being there. I believe we spoke briefly, but then I talked with so many people at that event."

"So you don't recall talking with us later?" asked Slim. "Afterwards?"

"No...I went straight home afterwards," answered the Egghead. "In bed before the ten o'clock news."

H.P. studied the dark circles under his eyes. "You don't appear to be well rested."

"I had a difficult time sleeping," the Egghead replied. "What with all the grief I've been feeling these past couple days."

Slim nodded. "Ah, because of your boss."

"That's right. Now I really must insist—"

"Wait, before you go, I want to return your coat." H.P. twisted slightly so that the burn marks on the back of the jacket he wore were visible. "I'm afraid it's a bit worse for wear, but it kept Ed warm last night while he and I waited for help. He's fine, by the way—just a little groggy."

"I don't know what you're talking about, and I'm sure I've never seen that coat before." The Egghead coughed. "I admit though, I am amused by you...the way you're talking now reminds me of one of those clichéd scenes in a suspense story during which the good guy gets the bad guy to divulge some incriminating information while surreptitiously wearing a recording device, but then I suppose authors like you need a vivid imagination to write such fanciful tales, though I imagine blurring the line between fact and fiction can be something of an occupational hazard."

H.P. pulled an eyeglass case from the coat pocket. "Indeed, over my career I've found that fact can often be stranger than fiction. Take a trope as tired as truth serum for example. Modern-day readers are much too sophisticated for that sort of thing...even if such a serum actually existed, say an amnesic developed in some diabolical laboratory, you just can't write it into a story—no one would buy it."

The Egghead blinked. "Do you really intend to use that on me? Try to inject me with that, and I'll scream bloody murder."

"Why inject what you can ingest?" Slim held up an empty syringe. "Besides, now all the serum is gone."

The Egghead looked down at his clean plate and blinked again. "You're too late. I placed the personal ad last night on my way home to run in today's edition, and this time next week the mosquitos will be breeding by the millions. Besides, anything I did tell you would be under duress and inadmissible in court."

"Then I guess I don't want to hear it." H.P. stood up and left the booth.

"But some of my law enforcement comrades might be interested in what you have to say." Slim waved over a man in a police officer's uniform and a woman in a dark suit who had been sitting at the counter. The pair sat down across from them. "Allow me to introduce the commanding officer of the two cops who've been keeping tabs on you since yesterday and a special agent with the FBI whose team, as I understand it, has had you on their radar for quite some time."

"I'm pleased to finally meet you in person." The woman set a small digital recorder on the table. "I have so many questions for you."

The officer leaned forward. "And, of course, this conversation is completely off the record, so nothing you tell us can be used against you…in a court of law that is. However, I'm sure anything a cooperative citizen such as yourself felt compelled to share would go a long way toward helping us build a case against a certain organization."

Slim put his elbows on the table. "And since all this information will be coming directly from the horse's mouth, which we'll be sure to broadcast in the appropriate channels, I imagine your buddies in that little organization of yours will shift their sights from Kate over to you."

The Egghead blinked once more.

Chapter 56

Weston did his best to look like he belonged at the funeral reception as he waited for an opening to approach the deceased's daughter. While she chatted with a group near the bar, he nodded at a few people who walked past. His mediocre celebrity status came in handy at such events, since people often recognized him without quite being able to place him, assuming—he imagined—that he'd been the old man's dentist perhaps or maybe a former caddy who'd come to offer his final respects for helping pay his way through college. Whatever they believed, they'd smile and continue on, not knowing him well enough to stop and begin a conversation but unconcerned that he didn't actually belong there.

Finally, Weston saw his opportunity. The daughter broke away from the group and crossed toward the kitchen. He caught up to her just before she left the capacious living room, tapping her on the shoulder.

She turned, knocking her glass against him and spilling wine down the front of his suit. She watched as the wine quickly soaked into the fabric of his jacket. Then she looked up at him. "They say turnabout is fair play."

"So I keep hearing."

"Come into the kitchen, and I'll get you a dishcloth to blot that with."

"Or maybe I can just take it off and wring it out over the sink." Weston followed her into the expansive kitchen, which was bustling with uniformed caterers who paid them no attention. "Is this the same staff from the last event?"

"I have no idea." She spotted a roll of paper towels on the counter and handed him a few. "If the arrangements for these types of things were left up to me, there'd be a case of booze set atop a card table next to a telephone and a phonebook opened to the food delivery section."

"That sort of setup would certainly encourage mingling." Weston dabbed at his jacket and the wine stain lightened slightly in color. "I think this is a lost cause, or at least a cause best suited for a talented drycleaner."

"Another use for that phonebook I mentioned."

"Your event-planning strategies are not without their utility."

"So what can I do for you, Mr. Payley, aside from hand you paper towels?"

"I thought you might be pleased to know that you were right. The man you pointed out yesterday was indeed the one I was looking for."

"I am pleased that he's been found out, though I take no pleasure in being right about such things. The thought of my dad's legacy being tainted by someone who'd committed wrongdoings under what might be misconstrued as the aegis of the company he founded is disconcerting."

"Yes, I'm sure it is, though I believe the perpetrator is being questioned by the authorities at this very moment."

"Good, then I trust this matter will be resolved soon."

"I believe it will be," said Weston. "However, there is another matter in need of resolution, and as it happens, it involves Aegis."

"You mean that million-dollar candidate for the glue factory, don't you? My dad loved that stupid horse, despite probably being able to outrun him—even with his cane."

"Ah...I was given to understand that Aegis is a world-class stallion."

"My dad was given that same understanding—by the shyster who sold the horse to him. Still, Aegis is a spirited animal, and Dad always was a sucker for longshots. That horse was practically the son my dad never had. He's scheduled to be sent to Gulfstream Park in Florida next week."

Weston rubbed his neck. "I see."

"So what sort of resolution were you seeking involving the shield of Zeus?"

"Regrettably, the sort along the lines of that gluey demise you alluded to a moment ago. We're fairly certain—almost positive, in fact—that Aegis was injected with a super-strain of malaria that may not prove pernicious to him but was engineered to be spread by any mosquitos that he comes into contact with, which could potentially result in a pandemic."

"You're asking that I have my dad's favorite horse euthanized on the day of his funeral?"

Weston sighed. "Well...it doesn't have to be today—just before next week."

"My dad's will explicitly stated that 'Aegis shall live out the remainder of his natural life running in the sunshine.'"

"I hate to even ask, but untold—"

"Iceland," she interrupted.

"Pardon?"

"Iceland has no mosquitos…and, during parts of the year, it's sunny nearly all day long. I can have him shipped there instead and still respect Dad's final wishes."

Weston grinned. "That's a very clever alternative."

"It's the sort of compromise that would've made my dad proud."

Chapter 57

Becky approached the ticket counter. "Excuse me, do you happen to know if the midnight train inbound from Birmingham is running on schedule."

The clerk quickly consulted her computer. "Yes…it should be arriving very soon."

"Would you mind also telling me if anyone else has inquired about that train in the last few minutes? You see, I'm picking up a friend, but I think maybe I got my signals crossed with a colleague of hers who might've also come to pick her up."

The ticket clerk scanned the rows of mostly empty benches in the station's waiting area. "The man in the suit sitting next to the door out to the arrival platform asked about that train a moment ago."

Becky pulled her sunglasses down from atop her forehead and looked over at the large man and then back to the clerk. "That's a big help—thanks."

"Sure thing."

Becky walked toward the exit, passing a teenager in baggy jeans who'd just entered. "The suit sitting at the far end."

"Then there's no need to whisper, Mom." Vance sauntered toward the arrival platform and looked expectantly out the window. Then he turned to the man in the suit. "Hey, what's good? Do you know if the train from B-ham is on time?"

The man looked up from his phone. "Do you mean Birmingham?"

"That's what I asked, boss."

"Yes, it's on schedule."

"Cool, cool," Vance tautologized. "So who you waitin' on?"

"I'm waiting for none of your business."

"All right, damn...it ain't that serious."

The man opened his jacket to reveal a pistol in a shoulder holster. "Is that serious enough for you?"

"Okay—just chill." Vance turned to walk away, nodding at a homeless man lying on a bench.

The tall homeless man stood and approached the man in the suit. "Spare any change?"

The man rebuttoned his jacket. "Beat it, you bum."

The homeless man continued to approach. "That ain't friendly. Not all us 'bums' are winos or dopeheads. Some of us just fell on hard times."

"You keep bothering me, and I'll show you a hard time."

"I was only asking if you had any change for the vending machine so I could get something to eat."

"I don't care what you say, all you bums are alike—nuisances...parasites."

"I can't hardly stand it when somebody assumes that because of my appearance I'm fittin' to act a fool." The homeless man reached into the pocket of his shabby coat. "It's shameful to derogate the underprivileged, but I bet you ain't never seen no bum with one of these before." The man in the suit eyed the police badge Slim held. "You shouldn't paint all us bums with the same brush, though I guess that's how it goes...guilty by association." Slim pulled his service revolver from his other coat pocket and the man raised his hands slowly. "Though you should know that it cuts both ways. I have a couple of my associates waiting outside who'd like to ask you some questions about your associates, but don't worry…they're dressed in real nice clothes just like you."

****

The train from Birmingham pulled into the station just after midnight. Edwin slowly stood from his bench as the passengers began to detrain. He spotted Kate and waved to her through the window as she stepped cautiously off the last car. She rushed in from the platform to greet him. "Eddie!" She hugged him so hard he nearly collapsed.

Edwin slowly retook his seat. "You're a sight for sore eyes."

She studied his face as she helped him sit down. "Your eyes look more tired than sore."

"It's been a long week since you left, but I'm very glad you're back."

"I'm glad to be back." She sat next to him on the bench. "Eddie, I've had a lot of time to think these past few days."

"You're always thinking…whether you have the time or not. It's one of the many things I adore about you."

"Eddie, in some ways we're so similar, but in others so different." Kate's eyes welled.

"To my tired eyes, your eyes look teary. Are you about to tell me that you don't want to be my girlfriend anymore?"

"The parts of us that overlap fit perfectly, and the parts of us that are different complement each other. I told myself that if we got through this, I no longer wanted you to be my boyfriend. I want you to be my husband."

"That means we'd have to get married."

Kate wiped her eyes. "That's usually what that entails...of course, only if it's what you want too."

"Would I have to wear a tuxedo?"

"We don't have to plan the whole wedding right now, but it would be helpful if you answered...preferably in the affirmative."

"Then yes, I will have you for my bride." Edwin moved to take a kneeling position on the floor.

"What are you doing?"

"I believe genuflecting is customary in these circumstances."

"Stop...you can barely sit without assistance." Kate helped him back onto the bench. "Getting down on bended knee is out of the question."

"As you wish."

"I like the sound of that better than 'I will have you.'"

Edwin smiled. "It's going to be a long marriage, isn't it?"

"It had better be."

Chapter 58

Edwin leaned on Kate for support as the two entered the Deluxe. "Oh Eddie, you take me to the nicest places."

"Really, I always thought this tavern was kind of a dump."

"I was being sarcastic. This bar looks like it ought to be condemned."

Weston approached the two. "We would've had you meet us at the Faculty Lounge like we planned on Tuesday, but the nice thing about here is that you're always pretty much guaranteed to have your run of the place."

Kate hugged Weston. "This looks more like a place one runs from, but I've spent the better part of this week holed up in a guestroom slash laundry room, so I'm just glad to be out in public again."

Edwin took a seat on a nearby barstool. "Don't go hugging her too tightly—she's soon to be a married woman."

Weston shook Edwin's hand. "So you proposed? I didn't know you had it in you."

Kate sat down next to Edwin. "Actually, I'm the one who did the proposing, though I suppose the salient point is that a proposition was tendered and accepted."

"That's not typically how the word tender is used when describing a marriage proposal, but it suits you two." Weston beckoned to Becky and Vance. "Come congratulate the newly betrothed."

Becky shook Kate's hand. "You're a very brave woman."

"Not really, I spent most of the week watching reruns."

Becky smiled. "Oh, right...brave for going on the lam too, of course."

Vance playfully punched Edwin on the shoulder, nearly knocking him off his barstool. "It looks like the stars have aligned."

Edwin rubbed his shoulder. "To what?"

"I don't know...it's just something people say in situations like this."

"Then may the stars align for you as well."

"Uhm...thanks."

Slim and H.P. moseyed over from the pool table. "It sounds like there'll be one less bachelor among us. I guess this proves there's an end cap for every telescope."

Slim patted H.P. on the back. "You should put that on a bumper sticker."

H.P. shook Edwin's hand. "I hear congratulations are in order."

"They are indeed." Edwin signaled to the bartender. "My good man, the drinks are on me tonight—but only for this group, in case any other customers should happen to come in later...and just soda for the boy."

The hoary bartender started pulling bottles from the cooler. "About time you bought somebody a beer."

Edwin turned to Weston. "I got an update from the others before meeting Kate at the train station, but how did it go with the heiress? Did you convince her to euthanize her father's prized stallion?"

"Nope, I couldn't talk her into it."

"What happened to your effect on women that you're always telling me about?" asked H.P.

Weston grinned. "Maybe I'm losing my looks. Perhaps someday soon I'll know what it's like to be you."

"So what then?" Slim asked. "Don't tell me we have to somehow arrange for an accident to befall that horse?"

"No, as I was listening to the poor, rich woman's pleas to find a way to spare her father's favorite steed, it occurred to me: Iceland."

"Of course," replied Edwin. "Iceland has no mosquitos—a most elegant solution. Why didn't I think of that?"

Weston placed a hand on his shoulder. "Don't beat yourself up about it, Ed. You've had a difficult week. Besides, we can't all be the smartest person in the room."

"Won't the horse get lonely there?" H.P. asked.

Weston shook his head. "I researched it a bit—turns out there are Icelandic horses. They're a little funny looking, which means he'll be extra handsome by comparison. Hanging out with you three, I can certainly relate."

"It sounds like felicitous news on all fronts then," said Kate.

"We got some good news too," added Becky. "Tell them, Vancy."

"Van, what's the word?" asked Weston.

Vance turned to H.P. "Come this fall, it looks like

you'll be seeing me on campus."

H.P. shook the young man's hand. "Well done."

Weston tousled his hair. "I'm proud of you."

"Thanks, but please don't touch my hair."

****

As the others played pool and drank at the bar, Becky and Weston danced closely in front of the jukebox. "So what's this 'effect on women' business that H.P. mentioned?"

Weston led them into a slow spin. "He's a writer of fiction...you can't believe anything they have to say."

"So by that reasoning I shouldn't believe what you're telling me now."

"I'd never lie to a woman as astute and intelligent as yourself."

"You're just full of it, aren't you?"

"Pants off to you for being so perceptive."

"I've missed you this week." She rested her head against his shoulder. "It'll be good to have you home again."

"Believe me, Becca, when we leave here, I intend to stay home for a very long time."

Epilogue

The moderator cleared his throat. "I believe we have a quorum, so I'll begin this virtual council meeting with the unpleasant task of updating you about the latest intel I've received. Our colleague who'd told us at the last meeting that the emergent situation we'd gathered to discuss was 'well in hand' spent a significant part of yesterday hemorrhaging information to law enforcement agents about the operation he'd taken point on, including the setting up of the overflow lab as well as the administration of the super vaccine. Evidently, he fell victim to the serum his personal lab had created, so we should assume that his every action and communication are now being closely monitored by various government entities, effectively ending his participation in this committee and most certainly rendering the operations he was directly overseeing an abject failure. Furthermore, I was just informed by the association coordinator that their organization is severing all ties with this council for what he characterized as 'gross incompetence' on our part. It seems in the last 48 hours, two of their operators killed each other, apparently in part due to the actions of our now-former colleague, and a third was apprehended by authorities after being sent at the behest of said colleague to retrieve the lab worker who managed to elude us for the better part of last week, which the coordinator called a dipshit snipe hunt—again, his words—that was a most disagreeable conversation. It now seems the aforementioned lab worker is the least of our worries. However, the one bright spot in all this is that I have already been contacted by a potential replacement for the member we've lost."

"That's not quite accurate," said the heiress. "I'm not seeking membership in this council, but rather I intend to offer the leadership it so clearly and desperately needs."

"This is outrageous!" replied a female voice. "The temerity of this upstart to presume to lead us is as shocking as it is offensive."

A calmer voice spoke up. "What we need now is new blood—not bad blood. How do we know she isn't trying to join our ranks in order to exact revenge for her father's demise?"

"She was the one who provided us with the information about her father's habits at home," the moderator said, "suggesting that we instruct the association operatives to take advantage of the time he spent alone each day in the stables."

"Dad and I weren't close, differing in opinion as we often did about how aggressive one ought to be when serving the greater good, which is why I didn't follow him into the family business. As for your disgraced colleague, he shared my outlook; however, he was myopic and sloppy. His plan to profit from a single vaccine was little more than a get-rich-quick scheme. Given enough rope, I knew he'd hang himself...and I was proven right. I assure you that my plans for this council are much more far-reaching, and now, with the two of them out of the way, I am well positioned to take over the company. The future is rich with opportunity for those who have vision and the will to act. So are you in or out?"

A word about the author…

Wesley Payton has a B.A. in Rhetoric/Philosophy and an M.A. in English. He has been a short-story presenter for the Illinois Philological Association. His play *Way Station* was selected for a Next Draft reading in 2015, and *What Does a Question Weigh?* was selected for a staged reading as part of the 2017 Chicago New Work Festival. He is the author of the novels *Lead Tears, Darkling Spinster, Darkling Spinster No More, Standing in Doorways, Raison Deidre, Oblong, Intimate Recreation, Downstate Illinois, The House Painter and the Pirate Hunter, and Immurdered: Some Time to Kill.* Wesley and his family live in Oak Park, Illinois.

Weston and H.P. will appear next in *Namastab: Transition into Decompose.*

Find out more about Wesley and his books here: http://wespayton.weebly.com/